Hotshot

Romance

Lira Brannon

Cypress Knoll Press
Cookville, TX 75558

This is a work of fiction.
Names, characters, places,
and incidents are the product
of the author's imagination or
are used fictitiously.

Printed in the United States of America

First Printing, 2017

ISBN: 978-0-578-19357-1

www.Lirabrannon.com

DEDICATION

This story is for the people who refuse to conform to the constraints of the norm and drop everything to follow their dreams.

To the transporters of every type that keep America's shelves and lots stocked.

Other Books By Lira:

A Different Kind of Cheerleader

A Different Kind of Black Belt

Four Days to Fusion

How to Eat Like a Dragon

To see what's next visit:

www.lirabrannon.com

Hotshot

Romance

CYPRESS KNOLL PRESS

CHAPTER ONE

Jill paused before the entrance of the driver's training room, hand hovering over the hard metal knob. Yet another solid partition blocked her way. There seemed to be so many lately. For the millionth time she asked herself—Can I do this? She'd come so far. *Just open the door, Jill, how difficult can it be? The hard stuff is done– you've quit your job, let the lease go, packed all your stuff. Just open it already!*

Smiling at the tough inner voice, she shook her head. Just one thing left to do. She closed her eyes and sent a quick prayer to the One who'd been there through it all.

That should do it then. She adjusted the one shoulder backpack and patted the reassuring bulge of her pint-sized Bible peeking from the handy pocket of the extra wide strap. The bag contained all the necessities for a three to four day trip—two changes of clothes, socks, toiletries, laptop, log book, and temporary plates. Tucked under her arm like a pig-in-a-blanket, her thermal sleeping bag cinched around her travel pillow.

Despite all the prep, prayer, and vacillating, she still could not stop her trembling hand. It skidded off the handle twice. Growling, she grasped it hard and pushed. It didn't move. She leaned into it, putting her shoulder against the chilly barrier.

Her sweaty palm slipped with that first fateful step forward. With a "whump", the heavy metal flew open from the combined pressure of her body weight and finally getting a grip on the reluctant latch. An echoing, nerve wracking crash heralded her arrival as the door slapped against the whitewashed haddock brick wall.

She fell in an inglorious tangle of arms, legs,

and sleeping bag. *So much for a graceful entrance.* Her glasses tumbled onto the hard, linoleum floor with a tinkling sound that made anyone who needed glasses, cringe. Her head cracked hard against the knobby knee of the lanky occupant of the last desk.

Fuzzy stars danced the tango in front of her eyes as she tried to focus. Nothing worked, yellow sunbursts blanked out the rows of faces turning to stare. She blinked a few more times, commanding her nearsightedness to work. She patted the floor. *Where were those wayward spectacles?* Her fingers touched the pointed end of someone's foot.

The spots grew smaller and disappeared, only to be replaced by the most outrageous crimson, knee-high cowboy boots with ornate stitching and the brightest yellow vamps she had ever seen. She squeezed her eyes tight again. Maybe she'd fallen into the wrong room. One could only hope.

Peeking up she caught a glimpse of eyes the color of a stormy winter sky, and just as cold. A long fingered hand, looking more suited to playing classical piano than driving, proffered her the missing, albeit twisted, eye wear.

Stuttering an apology, she slapped the offending frames to her face and scrambled to her feet. Even standing she stood dead level with those flat, blue orbs, shadowed by a shabby hat in almost comical contrast to the gaudy boots.

The cowboy touched his fingers to the nappy brim. "Ma'am." He turned towards the front of the class, dismissing her presence and fall. But he was the only one.

Her gaze followed his. "Oh."

Twenty-six pairs of curious male eyes examined her from all sides. They seemed to size her up, speculation bright in every one, all that is except the cowboy who refused to acknowledge her again.

She squared her shoulders. She'd been warned by her recruiter, Sam Vick, to expect things like this –maybe not falling into the training room on the first day—but the curiosity and dismissal of other drivers. Although the number of women in the trucking profession rose every year, they were still relatively few among the ranks of the hot shot drivers. And, she supposed, most of them didn't make such a conspicuous entrance.

Hot Shots of any gender didn't get the respect eighteen wheelers got as they ran their one ton trucks coast to coast. The loads they carried were not as large as the semi's, but just as varied. A driver could run from Texas to Indiana with a stack of flat bed trailers dragging behind and a load of car parts in the bed. Then they might turn around and shuttle between Indiana and Florida dragging an RV, then a boat from Florida to California carrying something else. They also didn't get the perks those big rigs got and were sometimes even run off the road by the bigger, more aggressive truckers. Few Hot Shots were female, but Jill knew this life was for her. It would fulfill her longing for adventure—and the need to hide.

Tossing her bag over her shoulder, she scanned the sterile room with blinding white walls. The floor, covered in a checkerboard of blue flowered linoleum, looked as though it belonged in her mother's bathroom. The variety of desks reminded her of an auction barn. All eras of schools were represented. From wooden single desks in the back, to a large rectangular metal desk shoved against the side wall, to short tables near the front.

A dry erase board shared the space in the front beside a large map of the U.S. The room was wall to wall men, all squeezed into desks meant for children. Despite the high pitched whine of a window air conditioner, a trickle of sweat slid down her temple. The room stunk of B.O. and testosterone, like gym clothes left in a hamper.

The only seat open was next to the taciturn cowboy in the rear. Shuffling against the wall behind him, she dropped her sleeping bag where she hoped it would be out of the way, as she went. She slid her bag against her knee as she scooted comfortably into the child's school desk. Patting it for reassurance, her heart skipped. The Bible was gone.

She peered around the fresh scratches in her glasses. Good thing she'd had the foresight to order a brand new prescription of ultra lights before she left. The cowboy, long legs stretched out before him, sat up as though stung.

She leaned over the desk to see what had captured his attention. Her Bible. She reached, her armpit coming up hard on the edge of the desk. No way could she reach it without drawing a bunch of attention again. Not enough room to get out and go around. Should she ask the cowboy in the blinding red and black stripes and pearl snap shirt to have a try?

She glanced over, but his jaw seemed clenched like she ticked him off. She rubbed the spot still throbbing from banging his knobby knee. No, she'd best leave him alone for awhile. He certainly didn't look like the friendly type. No matter how hat tippingly polite he seemed.

She leaned and reached forward again at the same time he did and found herself once again the center of unwanted attention.

***

King sized up the half-pint woman beside him. The recruiters must have chicken brains to keep hiring these lead footed female drivers. They all came in so big and tough, thinking they had what it took to make it on the road. This one had a cuteness about her that would have these fools eating out her hand and scrambling to find her the best loads. That there was reason enough to take an instant dislike to her.

He placed her on on the kind side of fifty, but still over the half century mark. Velvet brown hair, lightened with red streaks from the sun and a springy strands of gray, glinted in harsh florescents. Eyes the color of chocolate on a s'more lit by firelight peered hesitantly through thick glasses perched on a tiny snub nose. He shook his head, freckles too. But cute wouldn't cut the road tar.

She seemed upset about something, twisting and reaching in her desk, not that he blamed her, the tiny contraptions were more designed for torture devices than learning. He pinned his eyes on the U.S. map covering the whole wall of the tiny room, trying to ignore her fidgeting.

Dwarf Lady squirmed again, and then he saw

it. Right next to his hand-made boot lay a five by nine black book. *Must be hers*. Little gold letters glared up at him. His shoulders drooped and he shook his head. Flippin' flap jacks! Not only was the new driver a woman, she was a Holy Roller. Bet she couldn't wait to spread her faith across the country, converting lot lizards, drug dealers, and Hell's Angels. Every training session there were more. Itinerant preachers, wanna be soul savers— they never lasted long, but they sure could make life miserable for the old timers.

Sighing, King tried to curl himself around the torture device called a desk to reach for the book, just as the woman decided to duck underneath her own. Her fingers brushed his over the worn, faux leather cover. Static electricity popped. He jerked back, causing her to pull away as well and thump her head on his desk. The combined momentum upset his own chair. Out of control, he tipped forward. Grabbing at anything to stop his fall, he snatched at the desk, managing to snag the books the woman had set on the edge. In a flurry of pens, permits, and log books he tumbled to the floor–hard. Red boots stuck straight in the air like a caution flag.

For the second time in five minutes, all eyes turned to the back.

Sam, the florid faced recruiter for Sea2Sea and the closest thing he called friend, cleared his throat. "King, are you and Miss Mason about finished?"

Upside down and unable to give the instructor the proper glare he needed, King struggled to shimmy out of the desk. So it was *Miss* Mason instead of whatever her first name. Already special treatment for the woman. He ignored the outstretched palms of the helpful, smirking drivers handing him the scattered materials. He sent a particularly caustic look at the recruiter. The other man, in turn, openly turned aside a guffaw.

"I'm just fine, *Mr.* Vick. Thanks for askin'. You might ask *Miss* Mason if she's finished droppin' and tippin'. Mayhap you should get on with impartin' your useful information to these newbies here so we can hit the road." King cringed at his voice. His drawl, once likened by his mama to the rumbling of the thunder as it reverberated through the West Texas hills, sounded low and mean. It scraped across raw nerves, dripping with the utter contempt he held for all new drivers and this class. Men snickered.

Sam watched him struggle into the desk, then turned back to getting the class under way. Embarrassed at his teenage-like outburst, King handed the blushing Miss Mason her papers and log books then searched for his own. Talking to Sam like that was beneath him. The recruiter had been a good friend, no the best, through some bad times.

He tried to ignore the brief glimpse of pity he'd seen reflected on Sam's face. It made him want to hit something. But that kind of thing had gotten him in trouble in the years after his family had died. He couldn't go back there. Instead he groused under his breath until the drivers in the row ahead leaned forward as though fascinated by every monotone word.

The woman beside him, trapped against both the

rear and side walls, shrunk in her seat, swinging her legs nervously like Waylon on the way to the first day of kindergarten. King winced away from the memory, then stopped his mumbling. He shouldn't take it out on her, though it was her fault. She seemed so small and gave off an air of timidity and helplessness. It annoyed him.

"Settle down," he growled after a break in Sam's long winded welcome speech. "You're wound tight as a Texas rattler."

Chocolate eyes blazed at him. "Only because I'm sitting next to a king snake." She wasn't helpless. No, she was angry—at him of all things.

Wordless, King gaped at her. Why would she be mad at him? She'd tossed him out of his chair after all. Made him flip everything all over the room. Not the other way around. A tight silence stretched, broken by the squeak of the dry erase pen up front.

A burst of air escaped from Little Miss Short Stack. He jerked his head and stared as a giggle followed. Did she dare laugh at him? She slanted a look his way while keeping her face forward. She covered her lips, but he could see the smile curving her cheeks into little round plums below her bent glasses.

Nobody laughed at him. Ever. He valued his reputation as the taciturn go-getter. The one driver a dispatcher could call at the drop of a hat because he had no family hanging around his neck wanting him home. But no one got friendly. No way. And he liked it that way. Yet here she sat, practically rolling on the ground, tickled pink by her little joke.

Nasty words leaped to his lips, cruel sentences designed to put her in her place. Smother that laughter forever. Then she looked at him and the unkind phrases died unsaid. Heat crawled up his neck. He faced Sam again, unable to describe what made him stop. Best avoid this woman, she'd cause nothing but trouble in his carefully constructed routine.

CHAPTER TWO

King groaned as he watched the new recruits struggle over the log book problem on the board. Couldn't they see all it took was a few lines on that day's sheet? But no, hands shot up everywhere and whiny 'I just don't get it's echoed around the room.

Sam did the best he could, running hither and yon answering the same inane question again and again. Of course, King wasn't the only current employee in the safety class. Policy required every driver to take a refresher course once a year. Supposedly it kept them caught up on all the new safety regulations and policies, but after five years it got old. It seemed like the majority of the new material was a boatload of D.O.T regulations for equipment maintenance and less driving time to pay for them.

To top it off, new recruits just didn't understand log books. Most had high school educations which obviously hadn't taught them to tell time. Some older men, mostly retired big rig drivers, leaned back in the uncomfortable desks and went to sleep. Truckers became good at checking their eyelids for leaks whenever the opportunity arose—no matter how awkward the position.

No way could he try catching a nap. Not only was he crammed into the twisted metal desk built for a midget, now sporting a slight tilt from his earlier tumble, the woman next to him hummed a tune under her breath.

She glanced from board to log book. "Nope, that's not right is it?"

Is she talking to me? He looked down at the smudged paper then back at the board. "Not if you're looking at the problem up there. No." He cringed as she tore the paper off, tossed it to the small pile next to her, and started again. D*idn't she* *know never to tear a page out of a log book, ever.* That's a sure fire way to get D.O.T crawling all over a truck for a full out inspection and the company scrutinizing every piece of paper turned in.

He considered telling her, but figured she had to learn the ropes the hard way. She took the ruler to the mutilated log book. At least she drew straight lines, the transportation authority appreciated those things, but the hours didn't add up.

She drew a line in the top box for off duty from midnight to 5:45 then dropped down to on duty not driving for the 15 minute pre-trip inspection. So far so good. He cursed at himself for noticing.

Forcing his attention elsewhere, he scanned the room. A father and son team turned in their papers at the front of the class, then walked back, arguing each short step about one of the stops. That team didn't look like it would last long.

Two young men, fresh out of big rig training without finding jobs, sat back looking smug.

Sam kept busy with a group of five others and

one of the older drivers had been roped into helping. Others worked quietly, no closer to being done than anyone else. He looked back down Miss Mason's paper.

She'd carefully drawn her line to driving between 6:00 and noon just fine, but a trailer drop and a fueling stop had been run together when there was supposed to be a 15 minute drive in between.

He couldn't help himself. "Nope."

She growled and blinked up at him through bifocal lenses. "What now? What did I do?"

He shrugged, wanting to push his log book out of sight like a third grader. "Ask Sam. It's a common problem."

"Oh. Sorry, I didn't know you were stumped too." She raised her hand before he could sputter an answer. Him stumped? He could do log books in his dreams, and often did.

The instructor looked up in exasperation. "King, could you help Miss Mason?"

"I didn't hire on as a trainer," he snapped.

Sam glared at him over the bent head of a

scribbling newbie. King motioned to the flashing pencil. Groaning, the trainer covered his eyes. "No, no. Stop–" Another terrifying rip of a paper. "No, don't tear it out either. Please, people. You can't tear out log sheets. King, please." This time his voice whipped with frustration.

A blue shirted man struggled out of a far corner. "I'll help her." Stu, another driver in for his yearly torture. However, he was trapped against the opposite wall by several desks and long legs, he wasn't getting over here any time soon.

Besides, King didn't cotton to Stu. Not that he liked anyone. He waved the other man away after a quick glance at the recruiter. He knew the signs from years of working with the man, the short fuse burned near the end.

Sighing he turned towards the woman.

"Bless you," she breathed.

"Stop right there with blessings. Don't need 'em, don't want 'em."

Miss Mason jerked in surprise and he felt a sense of sad satisfaction. But it had to be said right off, to keep people off their Jesus soapbox. Especially if they learned what had happened. But he kept his past to himself.

"Now look, there's five hour rules you need to know. The 10 hour, 11 hour, 14 hour, 34 hour, and 70 hour. Actually, there's a 60 hour too, but don't worry about it. The 10 and 11 are this–" Wow, couldn't get much better than his condensed version of log book rules. That explanation needed to go the driver's training manual as the most concise explanation of a bunch of stupid rules ever.

He looked down at Mason. "Got it?"

She sat as though stunned, eyes glazed, mouth slightly open, pen frozen above her log book. Then she blinked and seemed to come back to the present. "Not at all. In fact, I think you made it even more confusing than when Mr. Vick explained it. I didn't think that possible."

How could she not get his explanation? He shook his head. Nope, definitely no hope for this one. He tried again anyway.

He curled his body towards her log book and

jabbed at it. "Okay, you drew your line here to off duty; drop down here to pre-trip for 15 minutes then bump up to driving until noon."

"Yes, I got that."

"Yeah. I know. That's the easy part. Now Sam likes to throw in a few harder things, but it's pretty close to real life. At noon you're going to drop the load, so go back down to on duty not driving for 15 minutes..."

After three more minutes of explanation and two new board problems from the ever hopeful trainer, she finally uttered the enlightening "I seeee." Swiftly she drew the marks on her paper. He glanced at her bent head.

Yep, she'd gotten a handle on log books. A flush of pride quirked his mustache. He had to hand it to her. She caught on quick. The other newbies would learn the hard way when they were called in for the inevitable log review, but this one might avoid that, well most of it. Every one got a letter at least once.

She beamed as her book matched the lines one the board. "I did it."

He nodded. "That'll work." Then because he didn't like the hot flush of pride threatening to make him smile, he added "Just don't think there will be someone holding your hand the whole time. D.O.T gets bullish if those logs aren't filled in up to the hour when you hit a weigh station."

"Oh, I know. But thanks for the help. After you get past the long winded explanations and get some hands on, it's not so hard."

"Long winded explanations?"

"Yes. You don't work with people much do you?"

And here he thought he'd been doing so well. "I'm a truck driver, Ma'am."

"Well then," she gave a tiny wave. "You're better at showing than telling."

An awkward silence fell between them as they waited for the others to finish and tackle the next problem. At least it seemed awkward on his part, she seemed perfectly at ease, even swinging her legs from time to time, studying the course materials.

"Mr. King—"

"Just King. . .Loveless."

"Really?"

"You heard Sam."

"I thought it was a sort of handle, like King of the Road or Driving King, something like that."

He stared at her and she flushed the color of a fresh peach.

"Anyway, sorry I called you a king snake."

His lips twitched again. "It's not the worse I've been called by a long shot." She still looked uncomfortable. For reasons he couldn't fathom, he felt compelled to put her at ease. "I'm kinda partial to it."

She looked up and smiled. He looked away fast. Every emotion played across her expressive face and right now it seemed to be joy. He cleared his throat, reaching back into the past for those little niceties one said to people to fill in gaps of silence called conversation. Nothing came to mind. It'd been too long. Not enough practice. Besides, the woman seemed too happy for her own good anyway. Best not encourage her.

She broke the quiet first. "I'm Jill–Jill Mason."

He touched his hat, but still couldn't find any words. Good thing he didn't need to, she talked enough for two.

"I don't have a handle." She mused to herself. "I'll have to get a name, maybe Wild Jill, or Lightening… " Once again the urge to smile came over him. This female could ruin his reputation around Sea2Sea if he kept sitting by her.

She cocked her head and studied him, reminding him of a quizzical grackle, those curious Texas birds that got into everything. "What's your handle?"

He scowled. "I told you, I'm King. Hot Shots don't usually have handles unless they come from a big rig or have a CB."

"Wow, I thought everyone had a nickname of sorts."

"Don't believe watcha see in movies."

She smiled. "Oh I don't. I suppose it works for you. It's unusual enough." She quieted down as

Sam ordered everyone to take out their D.O.T manuals. But a handle for her kept jumping into King's head. Sunshine. He shook himself. Focus, King. Thankfully Dwarf Lady sat pleasantly quiet until the trainer called a lunch break.

***

Jill left all of her gear in the training room and headed out to find something for lunch.

Tow-away drivers, those owning or leasing trucks, pulled out in a roar of engines and diesel perfumed smoke. A hand touched her shoulder and she turned, surprised at the surge of disappointment when it wasn't the tall cowboy with the blue/gray eyes.

The other man who had offered to help her on her log books stood grinning down at her. Stu, she remembered in a rush.

"Hey, you want to grab lunch before we hit the grindstone again?" He was a tallish man, but then again she'd never met a man that wasn't, with shoulder length blonde hair held back in a short braid. Faded jeans and T-shirt pulled tight over a thickening middle completed the look of a fading hippie.

"Uh, okay. I'm not really sure where I was headed yet."

"My truck's just over there. I'll show you around some. I've been to these things for five years now."

"Five years. You've been at this a while."

He grinned. "Yep. 75,000 safety miles. There's a place down in Nappanee that serves Greek food– gyros and stuff."

Jill smiled. "Sounds great. I like different foreign cuisines."

"Yeah, me too. Chinese, Mexican. I've tried them all. I'm Stu Wilson, 'case you didn't catch that, but people mostly call me Wayward Will."

She laughed. "King told me Hot Shots don't have handles."

She followed him to the charcoal Ford dually he pointed out and climbed up, happy for the chrome running boards. She nearly gagged from the pungent odor of working man as she stepped up. She used her foot to make a place for her feet in the piles of greasy fast food bags, old log books, and a few tools. Her bag with her wallet rested heavily on her lap.

Stu didn't seem to notice. He started the engine and pulled out of the yard. "King's got a reputation around Sea2Sea. You should shy clear of him."

She frowned. The cowboy didn't give off a bad vibe. "What kind of reputation?"

He turned onto Wabash Road so fast she hit her shoulder against the window from her precarious perch on the edge of the passenger seat. He didn't have an answer for her until he hit highway 19. "He's got a truckload of issues that keeps getting him in trouble. Rumor has it he spent time in jail for pounding some poor smo."

Jill's heart froze. She didn't put much weight in rumors, but when things such as violence to other people was mentioned, she sat up and paid attention. Hadn't she learned the hard way you just never knew about people? It was always those closest to you that caught you by surprise.

I need to be careful around these truck drivers,

she reminded herself. Friends and family often told her she was too open, trusted too much. But it was in her nature. Her mother always complained about her penchant to give people more chances than they deserved, not matter how many times she got hurt. Told her it was her fault for her two failed marriages and wayward kid. She cringed away from that last thought.

And here all morning long she'd been sitting next to the type of character that once upon a time came close to shattering her faith. To top it off, now she sat in a stranger's truck headed who knew where. At fifty-three years old she should know better.

She bowed her head against the window. All pain in the past had been mostly due to her not listening to the warnings of her heart. She had a blind spot the size of a black hole when it came to the people she loved. No matter how they abused her trust.

She remained silent, letting Stu ramble about the job, the drivers, the dispatchers, mostly all of it negative, but it washed over her without registering. Her heart thumped painfully in her chest. She spent all of her lunch second guessing the decisions that lead her here.

***

King ground his teeth as Jill climbed into Stu's truck. What kind of naive woman would just take off in a truck with a man she didn't know? He'd wanted to stop her, but then he didn't know why he'd want to do such a fool thing. He turned away —none of his business.

He definitely didn't want to take her to lunch. Besides, he couldn't figure why he worried. Stu had been part of the company for as long as he had, maybe longer, despite his lack of significant safety miles. He couldn't put a finger on why the other man rubbed him the wrong way. Perhaps it was the way he kept eyeing Jill, like a buzzard spying a newborn calf with a weak heifer. If he was her, he'd be hightailing it the other direction. Not climbing it into the other guy's truck.

Of course, if he was her, he wouldn't be sitting

next to himself or talking to him either. He most likely had a history far worse than Stu's.

He dug in his cooler for the groceries he'd picked up earlier. He just needed to settle down and avoid the woman. Like the rest of them, she could be nothing but trouble.

A man needed to stay focused, working, and not worrying about a female without a lick of sense. Yup, that's just what he'd do, pretend she didn't exist. He bit the end off of a granola bar. She did have a kind cute laugh though, the cross between a rabbit sneeze and a horse snort. He shook himself. Oh yeah, the woman had trouble branded all over her.

CHAPTER THREE

What surprised him the most was the woman's aura. It surrounded her like the welcome atmosphere of a home town honky tonk. He felt comfortable with her. So many times over the years, whenever he'd come in contact with other people, he'd get itchy all over, like he'd been standing in a fire ant hill—he couldn't get away fast enough. But he felt nothing of the sort with Jill, her presence was a balm in the testosterone riddled crowd. Her soft jasmine scent — Perfume? Soap? Competed with musky BO, aftershave, and cheap cologne.

So by the second morning when, like the creatures of habit people were, everyone took the same seats as the first day, King didn't mind when she sat next to him. The only change was Stu. Somehow he managed to switch seats with Sleepy Seb. The old man merely moved to the other corner and seemed to like it better because he slept the whole class. How the old geezer put in the million miles the numerous coat patches on his jacket proclaimed, he couldn't fathom. But the switch annoyed him.

On the third day, King arrived in the lecture room early as usual, not hard when he spent the night in his truck 100 feet from the training room, and propped his feet on the desk ahead of him.

As predicted, 15 minutes before class time, the door banged and a shadow blocked the light. A pencil tapped his boot. "Move it."

King didn't even lift the hat from where it rested over his eyes. He'd know Stu's heavy Old Spice aftershave anywhere. "Sit elsewhere. Plenty open still."

Something nudged his boots. "I like the seat by the corner."

"No need to fill up tight." Completely true. They'd already lost five from the class. The two boys had been called by a trucking company, one's wife had gone into labor (costing a half an hour of class time in congratulations and other hoopla), and the last two just never showed. Typical.

Stu stood over him for a moment then slunk away. A second later the desks screeched and the other man plunked down two seats away. The sneaky rat caught him looking and smirked. He shrugged.

The others came in by ones and twos. The guys were easy with each other now, calling out names and swapping road stories over lunch and during breaks. Some were even planning to run team already. That worked well for the drive-aways, those people who drove the RVs and buses. They often ended up some place without a ride. Renting a car with as many others as could fit would split the cost of the return trip. He'd tried it a few times, before he'd made enough to get his own truck, but he definitely didn't like the end of the line when he had to figure out how to get back to the yard. More than once he'd spent more money getting back than he made on the trip.

***

"Hey, Man, could you do me a solid?"

King stared at the speaker. *What truck had he fallen from?*

Marion, a dispatcher for the drive-away division, leaned against the wall like it's only support. He squinted in the florescent lights, eyes red rimmed and dull. Rumor had it, the kid kept himself sane by taking hits on the brown bagged bottle chilling on the ledge outside the service door. Looked like he needed another drink. Then again, maybe he'd had too many already today. Either way, he best steer clear of him.

Word filtered down through the mill that management had their eye on him. That was never good. At this rate he wouldn't be around much longer, at least not long enough for a collection on favors owed.

Curried goodwill was important in this business, particularly those between drivers and dispatchers. A good relationship with the person with access to potential loads gave a driver a slight edge. Could be the difference between getting a re-load, a paying load back to the yard, or dead heading. It could mean the difference between getting dispatched to North Dakota in the dead of winter, or Florida.

For drive-aways it got worse. A delivery could end up in the middle of nowhere with no way to get back to the yard except by their wits. A commodity in short supply among some drivers. Cities with little public transportation were more difficult. Entire profits could be lost trying to make it to the next load—as he well knew. Most drivers tip toed around the load masters, some even tried bribes of flowers (for the women) and beer and pizza (for the men) until the company made a policy against it.

King kept it simple. He used his 600,000 safety miles and five star rating to access the electronic load board–an earned privilege that allowed him to self dispatch. He'd gotten his passcard, and hauled a load into Canada once a quarter. Seldom did he talk to a dispatcher, and when he had no choice, he pulled rank and called Sam. Martha signed his dispatch papers, but he'd only nodded at her when he couldn't dodge the older woman in the short hall from drivers' room to the front door. No human interaction, no useless chit chat. Just work. He liked it that way.

None of this explained Marion's misguided assumption King might help him.

He needed to nip this kind of behavior at the bud. "I don't do favors." He continued walking. What more could he say? He infused his words with enough rudeness to stop further conversation on the subject of favors. The guy could spread the word of King's incivility, guaranteeing others would avoid that kind of familiarity in the future. Win-win as far as he could see.

One o'clock loomed. If a driver didn't make the afternoon section of the safety class, the unlucky sod had to wait a whole week to retake everything. It happened at least once a month, a driver sidelined when his safety certification expired. No doubt about it, those ladies in the office would shut a truck down–the company's reputation with the Transportation Department could be damaged irrevocably. Besides, it didn't set right with him to be late—anywhere. Tardiness in any area of life set a dangerous precedent, especially for drivers.

But the alcohol must have pickled the kid's brain, because he didn't let it go. "Vick said to talk to you, said you'd help me."

King stopped like a dog on a chain. "He did what?"

"Uh huh, we've run into a jam with this big show order in Omaha, there's also a big UPS order to Arizona going out at the same time. I just have the last two needing delivered ASAP. We're swamped."

King shrugged and tried to step past the blurry-eyed man. "Not my problem. I'm tow-away. I don't do motor homes, and I definitely don't do UPS trucks." Had the dispatcher lost his mind? Who ever designed those brown parcel trucks was a sick masochist. Those brown monsters drove like something out of the 70s. No AC. No place to sleep but a metal shelf designed for packages. No way.

Like a drunken elephant, Marion moved to block his path. "I've got to find a partner for this new driver—"

"Look. I definitely don't take new drivers or partners."

"But Sam said–there's this woman–" The man's tongue caught and stumbled over the phrases.

He glared, neverminding the younger man didn't slow.

"Her name's Mason, I think, Jill. He doesn't want her going off alone just yet."

King growled. That sounded like Sam alright. Always acting extra protective over the women. Trying to ease them into the job gently until the shock of the realities wore off. Then they'd either stay or go. Most left.

But the kid seemed to take his pause as

encouragement. He leaned in close and leered in his face. The alcohol fumes swirled so thick that if someone struck a match the whole building would blow to bits. "Now I got your attention, huh? For an older gal, she's pretty hot, ain't she? Of course, after looking at you sorry schmucks all the time, any woman would look mighty fine."

King's hands itched. Why did men disrespect women? He'd been raised better, and so had most of them. He curled and uncurled his hands. Breathing deep. Let it go. Jill should learn to expect this sort of thing. There were men like Marion throughout the industry—worse even. But this was beside the point. None of this—repeat none of this— concerned him. He just didn't get why it got to him all of a sudden.

"What did Sam have in mind?" He growled.

Finally catching on that King didn't appreciate his comment, Marion fumbled though the papers mangled by his steak-sized hands. "The show stuff is all taken. Motor homes and whatnot—"

King swiped a hand under his hat brim where

the sweat beaded. "Of course they are."

"—but there's 2 UPS' headed to Arizona. They need delivered by Friday. Sam assigned one to Jill. He thought you might tag along with the other. It's a big one. Pays okay."

"They don't pay period."

Marion shrugged. "Will you take it?"

"Aren't there any tow-aways? I hate being stranded without a truck."

Marion glanced down and shuffled papers. "Nope." He wouldn't meet King's eyes. "Stu volunteered—" The dispatcher let the sentence hang.

Him again. Stu seemed to be popping up everywhere and it got on his nerves.

"He's tow-away too."

"I know. Don't bite my head off, Dude. Sam just seemed to think you'd want it, that's all."

"I'll talk to him." UPS and a new driver and a female? He needed to hunt up that conniving recruiter and give him a piece of his mind.

"Come on, Man, I've got to get these off my

board before I go home tonight," Marion whined.

King held up his hand. "Save it or find someone else. Besides, I have safety till 5:00. Hopefully you'll find someone by then. And lay off the booze some, will ya?"

Marion dropped his eyes and flushed red. King ignored him—the practical driving started at one, and he wouldn't miss it for the world. Newbies made hash out of Sam's complicated driving courses and he often needed plenty of help rebuilding it after each driver. He didn't feel anything leaving Marion behind, maybe the kid would have get to work for once.

Chapter Four

"Whooo hooo." The little 21-foot mobile home handled much better than Daddy's old tractor. Jill just pretended those little cones were the pecan trees she had slaved to plant in the hot Texas sun and any damage to them would be taken out of her hide. Besides, all the bells and whistles of this sweet vehicle made backing it something a four-year-old could master. She weaved through the cones backwards, laughing at the little truck's maneuverability.

Mr. Vick sat in the passenger seat and three other drivers were in the back, already having taken their turn at the course. The trainer's knuckles turned white where he gripped the armrest between them. "You may want to slow 'er down, Miss Mason."

"Yes, Sir, but please call me Jill." She slowed to a less hair raising speed, stopped, put it in forward and finished the course without a single downed cone. "This is great. I hope they all handle like this little cutie." She patted the plump steering wheel.

Sam cleared his throat. "Well, about that. I got you a UPS truck headed to Arizona."

Jill couldn't contain the big grin spreading across her face in anticipation. *Adventure, here I come.* "Great. When do I leave?"

"You pick it up tonight after class, or at least before 9:00 tomorrow morning. There's several headed thataway."

"Wonderful." Jill stared at Sam. What's with the nervous shuffling of his papers? He looked back at the other drivers. A dark flush climbed out of his collar and if she needed to guess–he looked down right guilty.

One of the backseat drivers, an older guy re-upping his safety, smirked at her, tobacco stained teeth flashing darkly in a sinister smile.

She turned back to the recruiter. "Okay, what's up?"

"Well, look at it this way. People who help with UPS trucks can come back and get any load they want wherever."

The guys unloaded out the side door and started howling. "Wow, Sam's gonna give her a UPS truck first thing."

"Yeah, that'll teach her what for, for sure."

Heat crawled up her cheeks, but the men continued as though the open door were closed.

"Well, women shouldn't be driving trucks anyway—but that's just brilliant. Those trucks mess your back up for weeks."

"You're such an old fogey. . ."

Jill cleared her throat after the men had gone. "What is this? The twenties?"

Mr. Vick rubbed the back of his neck and sagged against the seat. "Some truck drivers are stuck in a time warp. They see this profession as one of the last standing. One not yet invaded by women."

Jill stared at him, waiting for the punchline. He didn't laugh.

"Honestly?"

Sam smiled wryly. "They really do." He turned serious. "We talked about this before you signed on. You're going to run into plenty of trash talk. You can either roll with it, or let it drive you crazy."

Jill straightened her shoulders and patted the backpack containing her Bible. "I can do this."

Mr. Vicks's smile broadened. "That's the spirit."

"But, what did they mean? About the UPS trucks?"

"Well—" He began, but he didn't get to finish as a new voice interrupted.

"Sam, we need to talk!"

Jill and Mr. Vick both jumped as a tall cowboy filled the side door. "What's this about teaming UPS trucks? Are you crazy? Everyone knows those things are death traps."

Jill glanced from one man to the other; the roomy cab seemed to shrink to the size of walnut. King's presence filled it, anger thrummed through him from the glittering pale eyes down to those outrageous yellow and red boots. Could Sam Elliot be his hero?

Her mouth twitched as she thought of the lanky man as Jubal Sackett, and then hid her smile as the blue eyes flashed towards her. But what was this about deathtraps? She got the feeling Sam wasn't being completely upfront about this trip.

But the cowboy didn't give her a chance to ask.

"Well?!" He demanded.

Sam motioned to Jill. "King, this is Jill."

Jill waved, her smile sneaking out as he gave her his best Sackett glare that made her want to laugh out loud. "Hi, again." Sam didn't seem worried about poking the other man's buttons. So why had Stu warned her about his temper? He didn't seem out of control, just frustrated.

The standing man sighed in frustration. "I

know who she is, Sam, quit trying to distract me. What do you have up your sleeve?"

"A favor."

"I said this many time afore—I don't do favors."

"You do now, and you owe me."

The men glared at each other over her head and Jill decided this would be the perfect time to make her getaway. Sneaking by, she made a break for the training room, leaving Sam to the cowboy. It didn't stop her from wondering what kind of favor King owed Sam—or that she liked the way he filled a space when he entered it. To her surprise, the cowboy backed out of the little motor home so she could get by and offered his hand to help her down the steps. Her heart flip flopped at his chivalry. The touch lasted only a second before his eyes returned to the other man. But the feeling of his large hand on hers stayed with her the rest of the day.

***

King couldn't help but notice when Jill left, some of the sunshine did too. He hesitated, turning to watch as she left. The way the light caught the red in her hair drew his eye. The way her hips swayed... He jerked back, grasping at his anger and holding onto it like a drowning man. Sam's sly grin as he noticed King noticing Jill helped.

"Nice gal, isn't she?"

"I don't want to talk about Jill."

Sam shrugged and bent to gather his papers. "It's a good trip to Phoenix." His green eyes turned hard as he brought them to bear on King's own. "And you do owe me. I don't call them in much. But I am on this one."

Sam's words rang harsh in his ears. Of course, he owed the fast talking son-of-a-gun. The other man had pulled him out of an alcohol soused bout of self pity and gotten him cleaned up. He'd hired him on at Sea2Sea and every once in a while, when it seemed like the past would take him down again, his friend showed up like a white knight, bailed him out of jail, chewed him out, and got him going again. The recruiter was a friend like no other. But, darn it, he'd worked hard and earned every single one of his safety miles. These past few years he'd gone through two trucks and three engines learning to keep the pain away.

Sam watched him like a rabid skunk. "Your truck could use an oil change and some new tires. Everything could be done while you run this load for me and there wouldn't even be any downtime."

His breath exploded. "What?"

"Don't make me side-line you because your tread's too low."

King snorted. As if he could. His tread never got below ¼ of an inch even though the legal limit was 4/32. But by the set of Sam's jaw he wasn't budging in this and he knew the recruiter well enough that he wouldn't give in until King took this load. He could also be a stubborn mule at times.

He tried an appeal to the other man's better nature. "But come on, drive away? A UPS? It's not like there's not a whole class of graduating drivers just rarin' to go."

The other man shook his head with a grin that claimed the victory. "They're taken care of. Just watch out for her. Show the lady the ropes. You're one of the best we have. You know those log books inside and out and D.O.T protocol like it was first grade work."

King took a deep breath; the flattery didn't help much. Of course he was one of the best. He worked at it. Drove carefully. Took his time. Inspected everything top to bottom—be it trailers or paperwork.

But Sam had him. There wasn't much a bitter man like himself could do to be a friend—and if Sam honestly needed him, he'd be there. Of course, the Ol' Softie would go and call in a favor for a woman. Even if she was a bright ray of sunshine where ever she went. "Alright, but that's it, you swindler, we're even."

The smile never left the trainer's face. "Not even close, King Snake, but you can think that if it makes you feel better." He jumped out before King could sputter a response.

CHAPTER FIVE

Jill stared at the UPS truck. Could this get any more complicated? The brown box truck listed to one side, a tire so flat the rim dug into the deep gravel of the staging yard. Her body slumped. She never dreamed this new job could be so difficult. Maybe she'd simply gotten out of practice of learning new things. She'd read it became harder as a person aged, but had always scoffed such a thing would never happen to her.

So here she sat. Sore. Exhausted. Even worse, she hadn't even started driving yet. After gleefully retrieving her paperwork detailing all the information about her first load, she realized it looked more like a foreign language than some thing she'd spent the last three days learning. She had to hunt down someone to explain it to her, but of course everyone wanted to get their day wrapped up and had no time to spare for her problems. Thank goodness the helpful Stu stuck around to answer her questions or she'd still be sitting in the office. He'd even given her a ride to the staging yard where the UPS trucks waited.

After a half hour of trudging through the lot inspecting the serial numbers of every UPS truck out there, she came back to the guard shack to report it wasn't there. The smirking kid in charge of checkout then informed her she was looking at the wrong number, UPS trucks had their own forms and numbers which weren't covered in class. Someone might have mentioned such an important tidbit of information earlier. But she got it. This was how they broke in the new drivers–haha.

She finally hunted down the truck, only to discover its front left tire resembled her grandmother's crepes. Of course, the clock on her phone chimed six o'clock in an annoyingly cheerful tone one hour after the office closed. No one would be available to help her until morning—her first road trip stalled out before she ever got started.

Jill glared at the offending rubber. Stu had offered to stay when he dropped her off, but she'd thanked him and sent him on his way. He'd been helpful, but he tended to hover. He chattered non-stop until a throbbing in her head started to pound in time to the rise and fall of his voice. She'd let him go with one of his admonitions to stay clear of King Loveless, and any other bad sorts in the company. Many of which he listed by name.

Besides, this was *her* adventure. She could do this, from finding her truck to figuring out whatever else came her way.

Darkness crept from the barbed wired topped fences, bringing a melancholy that poked at memories best left undisturbed. She clutched her jacket tight and tried to calm the sudden racing of her heart. She lifted her head and took a deep breath, struggling to control the panic attack.

I'm not alone, I'm not alone, she chanted. She

never had been. She touched the lip of her Bible peeking out of the side pocket and closed her eyes. Gradually, her heartbeat slowed. When she looked around again the darkness didn't seem to stalk her from the shadows. The sun set, fading to a warm spring evening filled by the thick scent of freshly turned earth as a farmer across the highway finished readying his corn field for planting. Jill watched the tractor make the last few sweeps, allowing the peace to sink into her bones before turning back to the offending bit of rubber—still flat.

She kicked it—hard. "Ouch!"

"That never helps."

She screeched and whirled. Her loaded backpack unbalanced her. The foot doing the kicking slipped on the loose gravel of the yard. She headed for another landing on her bum for the second time in as many days if long arms didn't reach out and steady her.

Jill stared up into the familiar face shadowed by the black felt cowboy hat and smiled. "Thank-you, Jesus." Like an answer to an unspoken, secretly wished for prayer, he'd shown up at just the right time.

King's hands fell as though scorched. He tugged his hat even lower on his brow. "Now, I've told you afore. None of your religious stuff." His tall, lanky form cast a long shadow across the gravel.

Jill laughed, relief that he wasn't some sort of crazy making her a tad giddy—it didn't matter to her he got insulted by her religion or that whenever she smiled at him, he growled. He was obviously an answer to prayer. Whether he wanted to be or not.

"Well, you're some sort of angel at least. How else would you know I was out here?" She looked across the deserted yard. Perimeter lights clicked on one by one throwing the parking lot into a land of shapes and orange light shadows, as the gentle evening acquiesced to full night.

"The guard told me a unit had a flat tire."

She raised her eyebrows at him. "That's it?"

"He also mentioned everyone had left but you." He peered around. "You all alone?"

A sharp fear coursed through her–why would he ask? She took another deep breath. These talks to herself about being safer were making her paranoid. She nodded.

King sighed and shook his head. "You need to be more careful, Lady. Try not to get caught out in strange places at night. The yard is pretty safe, at least it's fenced and has a guard. But usually he's only halfway aware of who's coming and going. Some places don't even have those."

His gruff spiel on safety caught her unawares. Who would have guessed this taciturn cowboy had a kind heart? But she didn't need a lecture. She could do this well enough on her own. Besides, she'd live long enough in fear. This was an adventure. "Well, as I always say 'My God is my protection.'" She paused when he didn't respond. "That's in Psalms."

"I know where it is."

That took her by surprise too. He knew his Bible?

"But all the martyrs quote scripture. Never

helped them one bit either. You need to use your head. Not trust some far away God to take care of you."

He tugged his hat down till his face was hidden in the shadows, but not before she saw a deep sadness in the lines of his eyes.

She wanted to reach out, say something, but then the moment disappeared on the breeze.

He took a step back. "Come on, I'll take you to a motel for the night."

She motioned to the flat tire, "But . . ."

"After hours nothing happens around here unless you're willing to raise Cain. You can try to get the guard to help you, but I'd advise waiting 'til morning. The day crew moves a lot faster." He turned away. "You could try kicking the tire again, might blow up on its own."

So he did have a sense of humor–a dry one. Heat crept up her cheeks. "Well, it made me feel better any way."

She looked back. He strode towards the guard shack where his Dodge dually chuffed like a white tiger. She jogged to catch the bright red boots through the gloom, keeping at a trot to keep up with the cowboy's long stride.

He checked in at the guard shack. Told the kid on duty, who seemed a lot more differential to him, about the tire, then opened the passenger door. He paused, blocking it for a moment, as though his gentlemanly action caught him by surprise. For the second time that evening heat bloomed over her cheeks. Such manners. First helping her out of the motor home and now.

Jill hoisted herself into the cab. This time she found herself in a far different world than Stu's messy truck. The console lit up in the twilight, illuminating the computer station taking up the center seat and a quarter of the passenger side. Gadgets lined up like ducklings in front of her along the dash. She glanced behind her. A neatly made bed consisting of a sleeping bag over a foam mattress and pillows piled high against one door took up the whole back seat.

"Wow."

"Sorry about you not having much room. I don't get many passengers."

Jill twisted in the seat with a squeak of leather and the smell of lemon leather conditioner. The vinyl gleamed, even the vents didn't have the usual layer of dust most cars collected, and it was definitely minus the trash piled on the floor on the passenger side of Stu's truck. "This is nice, leather seats, chrome—it looks new."

"It is."

She raised a brow at him, encouraging the taciturn man to continue. He obviously took pride in his vehicle.

He glanced at her then focused on the road. "I bought it last year, the engine has 150,000 miles. I did replace the rear axle last month."

His voice rumbled like a water in the mountains, all powerful but soft, as though she listened to a waterfall from a distance away. She needed to keep him talking so she could hear more of it. She grinned at him. "There, that wasn't so hard was it?"

"What?"

"Making conversation."

He didn't answer.

She stroked the armrest. "You must clean it all the time."

This time he volunteered more information. "Sometimes it gets slow between loads, so I clean the truck, change the oil and coolant—that sort of thing. A truck runs better when it's clean."

"Of course it does. Do you have a home?"

His face closed. "You're sittin' in it."

"No, I mean like a house, a home base, somewhere to wind down, you know."

At first she didn't think an answer coming, nothing showed on his face as it flashed orange and black in the light of the blinker. "Not anymore. This here's it." His bass voice rasped even lower, filled with raw hurt and an 'I don't want to talk about it' tone.

She had trespassed too far. But she understood completely. Hadn't she put every last thing in storage and now carried all necessaries in either her backpack or car. Her parents thought she'd finally gone off the deep end. Her sisters openly ridiculed her. Nobody understood. Nor could they.

She stared out at the passing lights admitting that being passed over at work again was merely a convenient excuse, as was the fact Shawn had finished college and on his own on the West Coast, and then she told herself she'd always wanted to travel. These were all true, but to be honest, the letter had started it all. A simple one sentence missive from her daughter, Stacy, stating she had served her time and would be released within the year.

Jill looked down at her hands and then clasped them together to stop the trembling. She might tell herself God led in her life, and oh how she prayed that was true, but honestly she couldn't say.

The whole thing had struck out of the blue. Over a year ago she'd picked up her mail like any other day, discarding the ex's AARP stuff – still coming after nine years of phone calls and written explanations, and shuffling the bills to the back as she scanned for a letter from her Mom.

Her hand paused over a plain white envelope with a return address from Stacy Mason, Texas State Penitentiary at Huntsville. She'd stared at it for days and when she opened it the words were simple, "Mom, I'm getin out. Where are you?"

After ten years, her oldest child would be free, and she obviously still held her mother responsible. After all, Jill had turned her in, in a roundabout way. The judicial system had done the rest— charges for beating her mother near to death, lighting the house on fire to finish her off and hide the evidence. Only God had preserved Jill through the nosy neighbor always in everyone's business. He'd spied her struggling to get out the back door as smoke poured through every window. He'd helped her and called the police. Stacy, still at the front of the house watching it burn, had no idea Jill had made it out until the police surrounded her. Jill fingered the scar on her temple, hidden by her hair.

Guilt and worry crashed around her, threatening to consume her. Did she think this would work? Keeping on the road and away from any permanent place to keep her daughter from finding her? She didn't want to go to the police. She loved her child, despite it all.

Her first born had always been a violent child, large for her age and so determined. Nothing would stand in her way this time if she decided to finish the job. Her pulse jumped, panic threatened to overwhelm her. Not a panic attack! Not here, not now. She was over that. The therapist had declared her cured years ago. It had to be this change in routine, the increase of fear and uncertainty triggering a relapse. *Please God, help me.* Slowly her muscles relaxed. She unclenched her fingers from the armrest one at a time. She tried humming her favorite hymn, that helped, and focusing on the bright lights of the night.

"Jill?" King's soft draw broke her reverie, bringing her back to the present. The truck idled in front of a dimly lit motel. "You okay?"

She forced a wide smile to her face, feeling like a grinning wolf and hoping the semi-dark made it look better than it felt. "Yeah, sure." She fumbled for her bags. "This is great, thanks so much."

King looked like he might say something else. *Please, please, don't. Please don't ask me about my near panic attack. Please don't make me talk about this.*

"This motel has a discount program with Sea2Sea. Keep your receipt and the company might reimburse you since this is technically a breakdown."

She eyed the peeling paint and a sign with half the bulbs out, reluctant to leave the warmth of the truck and, despite his gruffness, the comforting presence of the tall man. "Oh, okay, sure."

"I'll pick you up in the morning. I have the other UPS truck going to the same place so we might as well get started early. How does seven sound?"

"Sure. That sounds great." Even to her own ears her voice sounded dull, energy drained from thinking about the letter. She knew no matter how tired she was tonight, no way would she get any sleep. She tried to keep certain doors shut in her brain. When they opened, even just a crack like remembering the letter, it haunted her. She dropped to the ground, bags landing with a thud at her feet, then trudged towards the hotel, too tired to do more than toss a final wave over her shoulder at her rescuer.

Chapter Six

King let the engine idle, watching to make sure his new partner made it to the lobby. The walk to the front desk could only be about 10 yards, but if her dragging feet and slumped shoulders were any indication, she was out of fuel.

Should he have carried her bags? Once upon a time he would have leaped out of the truck to do so, his mother's training of a southern gentleman, even a cowboy, ran deep. What happened to him? He brushed the thought away and hardened his heart. He didn't want to dredge up memories of the events that had shaped his life. Asking questions only brought back pain, then anger. It was only downhill after that.

Besides, the lady needed to get used to carrying

her own things. The doors swung shut behind her, he shifted to drive and headed back to the yard for the night. But his thoughts didn't leave the little woman.

What kind of secrets lurked in her past? She'd turned the color of a catfish's underbelly when the conversation turned to homes. Obviously the subject wasn't any dearer to her heart than his. What would frighten a Holy Roller? Didn't they just hand it all over to God and breeze through life without a care? Of course, Carol had tried that and look where she ended up. Her and his boy dead in the middle of some forsaken African village. Jill tried hard to convince him she didn't have a care in the world as she quoted the Bible at him. He shook his head. *She puts on a good front, but she's not as comfortable in letting God be in control as she wanted people to believe.*

***

Jill collapsed onto the lumpy mattress with a groan and lifted her feet straight to the ceiling. She couldn't feel her toes. After fifteen years of sitting on her rump with only running to and fro to the warehouse had left her twenty pounds overweight and out of shape. She took a deep breath of the brain cell killing, bleach scented air and immediately sat up coughing. She looked around at the putrid yellow walls and chintzy art and sighed. Now what?

This afternoon everything seemed to be falling into place. The road stretched out before her. All the little ducks lined up in a row. Get a load and get out of here. What could be easier? She never dreamed the amount of paperwork and fact checking that had to take place before she could even get in the vehicle. Then there was that blasted flat tire.

Desperation seized her. She needed to hit the road–now. The more she moved, the harder she would be to track. With shaking hands she reached for her Bible. She stroked the old cover, but didn't open it.

How could she? Everything up to now she had planned with the lie upper most in her mind that God willed this. But had He? What did He have to say about her fear and her running? If she opened the Bible, He would tell her in no uncertain terms. Could she face the truth?

She comforted herself with just touching it. Her mind focused on a verse she knew by heart from somewhere in Deuteronomy. 'The Lord goes before you. Do not fear, He will be with you. He will not fail you.'

Sighing she turned on her side. Despite everything, her eyes drifted closed. She didn't even have the strength to kick off her tennis shoes.

***

A pounding shattered the stillness, vibrating across the flimsy door and rattling the window, ending up directly in her skull. Could a headache shake down the cheap walls? Jill struggled from the abyss of exhaustion incrementally. Sleep glued her eyes into slits and she dug in the heels of her palms in to clear her blurry vision. She'd fallen asleep with her glasses on, the twisted frames felt glued to her skin. She shook her head. *Wow. I haven't done that in forever.*

Glancing around the room, mustard yellow walls, antique television on a chest of drawers from the 80s—she remembered—oh yeah, roach motel, utter exhaustion and frustration. Weak sunlight filtered through the plastic lined curtains. Good, still early. Maybe she could grab a shower before her ride arrived. She jumped with a shriek when the pounding started up again. That's not my head! She didn't even have a headache, though she should.

An obviously impatient someone beat at the door again. "Jill? You up?"

A smile found its way to her face as the deep voice rumbled through the closed portal as though the man stood beside her.

The she remembered—seven o'clock. Early start. She leaped from the bed. "Ow, ow, ow." Pins and needles electrified the soles of her swollen feet, still wrapped like sausages in her sneakers. She groaned and fell back onto the bed.

King must have heard her. He pounded again. "Are you okay?"

A charley horse took a hold of her leg and she

whimpered.

The knob rattled. "Can you answer me? What's going on in there?"

She reached for her calf, but her back muscles were short and sore from lugging her backpack the last few days and spasmed warningly. The knife of pain stabbed squarely in her lower spine and despite effort, she couldn't reach it. The knot in her leg intensified and what might have been a funny, little bit painful situation ignited into an inferno of agony. She hurt everywhere now. Tears seeped from squinched eyes and she fought just to breathe. If the pain wasn't eating her from the outside in, she might liken it to having a baby. Despite the agony, she smiled, but it looked like a grimace for sure.

A shaft of morning light flooded the room as the booted cowboy flung open the door with a force that shook the motel at least three rooms away. "Thunder sticks, Woman, what's going on in here?"

Embarrassed beyond speech, she rubbed at the screaming muscle, ducking her head to hide her face. Hands that were rough in hurry grabbed a foot and untied the laces to her sneakers. Fingers gentled as he eased the offending shoes from her swollen limbs. Circulation returned in a flood like a thousand bee stings as blood rushed through unrestricted vessels.

"Ouch. Ow. Ow. Ow."

"Just sit back. You should have taken your shoes off last night."

She laughed, but it turned out as a snort as her muscles clenched again. "You think?"

Knowledgeable hands wrapped around the epicenter of the muscle spasm, kneading in slow outward circles. The pain receded, bit by bit, and coherent thoughts intruded on the pleasant feeling of the leg massage.

She glanced at the swipe key on the bedside table. "Umm, I know this sounds ungrateful, but how did you get in here?"

King released her leg and marched the two steps to the tiny bathroom–a man on a mission, intent on the job at hand and obviously not registering her question at all. He returned with a damp washrag which he wrapped it around her calf. She sighed as the warmth finished untying the rest of the kinks. The cowboy straightened and backed towards the outside opening, as though coming to the realization he'd just broken into the room of a virtual stranger.

She stifled a giggle as his eyes shifted about the room, resting on anything but her as he explained himself.

"Motels like these older ones are easy to break into with a screw driver. I have an army knife on my key chain and tools in the truck if need be." He motioned to the gleaming white vehicle parked so close the bumper peeked through the gaping entrance. From this angle it looked as though the truck were bigger than the room. In an instant he turned, bright red staining the tips of his ears. "Don't you know to latch the chain when you stay in a room opening to the outside? Anyone with half a brain could force their way in. If'n you're dead asleep you'd never know 'til too late."

Jill cringed away from his tirade for a split

second before realizing his anger came from embarrassment at breaking into her room. Maybe even worry for her. *How sweet.*

She glanced towards the open door. "Well, at least you didn't admit you were a cat burglar in another life." The flush spread from his ears, climbing down to the the collar of his blue checked button down. "Usually I'm a light sleeper."

His blue eyes glared from beneath that nappy cowboy hat. "That may be, but it's nine in the morning and I broke into your room in two seconds once'n I put my mind to it."

"Nine!" Jill jerked her legs to the floor and stood, blinking back stars. "I thought you told me we were going to get an early start."

"Yes," he drawled. "I've been at the cafe since six. I decided check to up on you once I started on my third cup of coffee."

Jill skittered around the room, throwing her things into her backpack. "I am so sorry, so so so sorry." She hopped to the beat of her chant, trying to shove tennis shoes back onto sausage feet. With a huff she gave up and sat on the bed to yank out the laces. She then flew around the room.

The cowboy stepped well out of the way of the whirlwind dancing in her wake. She hurried to the bathroom two or three times, 'just to be sure', then looked under the bed and every single drawer before stopping half a second. She'd hate leaving something. Not that she'd unpacked any the night before, but the tall man in the doorway flustered her.

This looks bad, Jill, over sleeping the first day on the job. How could you make a good impression doing things like that?

She finally stopped to catch her breath. "I think that's it then. I'm ready."

He turned his head to study the geometric print on the wall and she looked with him. What could have drawn his attention all of a sudden? Didn't he want to get moving? His mustache twitched with a grin.

"What is it? Did I forget something?"

He adjusted the hat on his head and cleared his

throat. "You may want to brush your hair a tad."

"What?" Jill whirled to the mirror and shrieked. What once had been a pony tail on the back of her head now nestled by her ear like some sort of nest. The rubber band only held half of what it should have. The rest formed a halo of sleepy knots and wispy runaways.

She yanked at the elastic, wincing as she pulled out a tuft, leaving a tender spot. She threw her backpack on the bed and rifled through it. "I know I just put that brush in here. Aha!" She raked the bristles across her scalp.

A deep chuckle rumbled behind her. She looked at the cowboy out of the corner of her eye. He had his back to her, as though trying to hide the shaking of his shoulders. It wasn't working.

She faced the mirror again–so mortified she wanted to cry. Then she took a good look at herself. "I look like Shaggy run through a car dryer." The hilarity of the situation hit her. A guffaw escaped. Yep, that's exactly how Shaggy would look. She fluffed her hair then shook it out. Then she shook her head and the laughter bubbled out. She gripped her sides and reached for the bed for a sit down to catch her breath.

She shouldn't be laughing. How many times had the ex run her down in the morning? Say she looked like a bramble bush? It got so she made sure she rose early and looked presentable by the time her chronically unemployed husband rolled to the couch to start his video games.

King kept his gaze tactfully redirected. But it didn't stop his smile widening under his salt and pepper mustache. Then he joined her in the laughter he'd been trying to hide and he chuckled right along with her.

She gasped a breath, "Sorry about that. I'll get going, really. No wonder you wanted me to brush my hair. I looked scary." She choked back a giggle as she thought of Scooby seeing Shaggy like that. Yep, a horror cartoon in the making.

CHAPTER SEVEN

King nodded and faced outwards again with a deep breath. He had laughed. Out and out laughed for the first time in forever. His body felt lighter. A strange feeling he couldn't place stole over him. It seemed familiar, but its name eluded him. The bitterness that filled his throat every morning, eased. He forced himself to turn away from the softness in the room. He had no business to it. His heart ached and he shook his head. Guilt swept over him. Waylon. His mood soured again as it should. He had no right to be happy, not with his little buddy gone. The familiar ache darkened the day, it could not dispel that moment of forgetfulness when his spirits rose with the laughter of the little lady.

He sought for a reason to find fault in her joy. She *had* looked ridiculous. But her response had taken him by surprise. She'd laughed. What woman in her right mind would make fun of herself in front of a strange man? Carol's routine had included rising two hours to primp before she went anywhere.

While he thought, Jill turned back to him wiping tears of laughter from her eyes. "I love to start the day out with a good laugh."

He just stared at her, trying to figure the quick silver change. The driving industry got all types, but she seemed just a little off kilter. Probably would fit right in. The question burst from his mouth. "How do you do it?"

She shrugged as though her joy came easy. "Don't you love how God created laughter to brighten our days? Even when they start out with pins and needles and an incredible Charley horse. Besides, I had an ex who made my life misery until I learned just to laugh. You know the saying, 'a merry heart is good like a medicine'. Besides your talented hands, I think the laughter tipped the scales in my favor, don't you think?" Jill peered up at King as though trying to read his mood.

He fumbled for words. "No."

She ignored his gruff response. "I would have thought that you were a masseuse once." She grinned at him, trying to get him to laugh again.

He shifted uncomfortably with her attempt and turned away. "Come on—we need to get started."

He tried to speak with his customary surliness, but her smile widened. She waved him out the door. "Lead on then, oh Loveless Leader." She chuckled.

She's laughing at me again. But this time it didn't rankle like before.

***

The laughter worked wonders in lightening her mood. It chased away the last of the pain and the dark thoughts from the previous night. Good thing too. The morning didn't go as well as she thought it should. The remaining early hours were filled with making calls and getting her truck ready to go down the road.

All the while King took care of his own business, surprising her by claiming the UPS truck next to hers.

"I thought you're a tow-away driver."

He looked longingly at his truck parked against the back fence. "Sam pulled a favor. Looks like I'm headed to Arizona."

Nothing like the feeling like a bug under a magnifying glass. The cowboy hovered as Jill began her pre-trip. Finished with his own prep, he stopped to watch her.

Finally he sighed. "Want some advice?"

"Not if it's like your log book explanation," she teased gently.

He stared at her for a minute as though trying to determine if she were serious.

"Go ahead," she added.

He nodded. What should have been a 15 minute inspection turned into a 45 minute hands-on lecture. He showed her how to check the torque on the lug nuts and look for any scratches or dents that might be blamed on her when she got to her destination.

After working the truck over, he showed her the number on her paperwork for the number to phone in a breakdown. She made the call and in short order a UPS repair crew showed up and went to work.

Precious driving time passed, but despite the impatient reputation Stu warned her about, the cowboy never lost his temper with anyone. She tried to thank the man more than once– he was quickly becoming the God send she named him— but he just waved the compliment away like an annoying mosquito.

Other drivers retrieved loads. The lot emptied and then filled as the shuttle drivers got to work. Each time a driver honked and waved, she expected a flash of temper that hinted at a hidden character flaw. But he never did. She expected him to leave, to tell her he'd see her down the road, but he didn't. The other two men responsible for the last of the UPS trucks to leave the yard waved and hooted at her.

She checked her phone, it seemed odd that she

hadn't received her usual good morning text from Shawn. Her son always seemed determined to make up for his older siblings mess-ups and went out of his way to do nice things.

She fiddled with the buttons as the brown truck heaved into the air with the hiss of a hydraulic jack. Pneumatic tools beat a staccato rhythm of the roar of the motor homes and trucks. "Hmmm. I must have turned it off. Eight texts?"

Shawn: Hey Mom. Good luck on your first trip.

Then there were a slew from a new number. Stu.

Wayward Will: Sorry couldn't stay. Time is money you know. Have a good trip.

Wasn't it me who told him to go ahead and go?

Wayward Will: Haven't heard from you. Tire fixed?

Wayward Will: If you have questions just call me.

He could have pointed out the breakdown

number like King did. She grimaced at her unkind thought.

Wayward Will: Still no news. How's the trip? Let get together for lunch when you get back.

The texts went on and on. Sometimes two or three within a few minutes. *Creepy.* She'd just met the man and he texted more like a long time friend. She glanced at King. He stood tall as he talked to the crew chief of the repair men. He leaned forward slightly to listen to the smaller man. Then again, a man she just met had spent his morning driving her around, helping her, breaking into her hotel room. She sighed and rubbed her face.

No matter what Stu said about King, she just didn't get a bad vibe from the man, it was more like he was gruff because of a painful past. She well understood that. But the Lord had carried her through and though she back slid sometimes into doubt and fear, she knew He was with her. She just needed to communicate that to King.

She shoved her phone in her jacket. He definitely didn't want to hear anything about God.

Even the mention got him angry.

Her phone beeped.

Wayward Will: Where are you?

Me: Just getting underway.

She turned it to silent. Hopefully that would stop the texts for a while. King and one of the men seemed to be consulting about something, hunched over the damaged tire, pointing here and there. What could be so interesting about a flat tire?

At her approach, the two men straightened. King tossed the tire in the back of the truck. The other loaded his tools. "You're good to go. Have a safe trip."

She shook his hand. "Thanks."

She turned to King. "Now what?"

He pointed to the office. "Get your advance and let's hit the road."

CHAPTER EIGHT

The office echoed with her footsteps. A single driver sat in the corner staring with blank eyes at his phone. He never looked up at Jill's entrance. A light burned at the end of the hall. Most everyone had gone to lunch, but it looked as though the dispatcher, Marion, stayed to cover the hour. Jill peeked into his cubicle. He sat with his head on his arms. The sweet smell of beer filled the small space.

She knocked before she could change her mind. "Um, hi. I have some receipts I need to turn in for a breakdown.

The dispatcher raised his head, blinking rapidly as he focused through blood shot eyes. "Jill, right?"

She smiled, sidling into the office. *What's going on with this guy?* She hated the smell of alcohol. It reminded her of broken promises, pain, and fear. "Right." She gave him her driver number.

"Already with a breakdown?'

"A flat tire last night."

He motioned for her to come closer and sit in the tattered chair near the desk. She perched on the edge while he shuffled the receipt and then the request back and forth, peering at them. "Okay then. I'll turn it in. No telling if they'll say yes or when, so don't count on a reimbursement any time soon. When you leave the yard you'll get your 80% advance and you can fuel."

He waved in dismissal and she bolted. Her hand touched the flimsy cubicle wall, but the man's obvious misery made her pause. She didn't want to leave without a kindness spoken. So many times during the rough periods in her life a simple smile had made her day.

She glanced back. Sure enough, he'd dropped his head into his hands and stared unseeing at the desk.

Her heart prodded her to speak. "Umm, are you okay?"

He jerked up. "Yeah, yeah, I'm fine. Did you need something else?"

She motioned to the request he'd put in the top paper tray. "I handed in some paperwork."

"Oh, okay. I'll get to it."

She took a deep breath. "This place smells like you've been drinking. I thought I should say something, just in case someone came in and noticed. It might not look too good." She cringed against the door as anger suffused his face, turning his fair complexion to a mottled swirl of rage, then, just when she thought he would lunge at her he crumpled back into the chair with a sigh of defeat. She edged closer, once again finding a perch on the chair, trying to avoid the curled edges of the upholstery that poked her painfully in the backside. She waited for him to speak.

***

King stormed into the vacant office building. One o'clock had come and gone, way past time to be getting some driving in before dark. He glanced this way and that, trying determine where that woman had gotten too.

Becky, one the secretaries in the pay department, squeezed by him where he blocked the door. "Excuse me." She scuttled away as he scowled down without seeing.

She nearly reached the key coded protective door that kept the drivers out of the back rooms of the pay department when he decided to speak. Generally, all conversations with those employees were carried out through a thick glass window with a couple of holes at mouth level.

"Hey, Becky," he called.

She stopped, glancing at him then back towards the key pad, looking like a cornered rabbit. "Yes?"

"Have you seen Jill Mason around?"

Becky lost some of the nervous twitch most pay people got after a year or two. Why anyone would want to work in that difficult job he couldn't fathom. Some drivers went so far as to use them as verbal punching bags when it came to pay. For some reason Stu came to mind at the thought of those sorts of people.

"No, I haven't. I had to make a quick trip to the overflow yard at lunch and haven't seen anyone." She whirled and darted into the safe zone before he could say anything more—like ask about money. Come to think of it, he did need a new pay card. The plastic tended to get brittle over time. Silence fell on the office except for a small buzz from the far end of the hall. Curious, King headed that way, having a hunch as to where to find Jill.

The buzzing turned into voices as he got closer to the last cubicle on the left. He stopped just outside the doorway, listening for Jill's soft speech. Sure enough, she talked in low, soothing tones, like those used on a child. He peeked in. The object of his search sat across the desk from the drunk dispatcher.

"I can't say I know what you're going though, but I have kids, so I know it's bad when one of them is hurt. You'll get through this. I know you will."

"But Kelsey's just a baby, she wants to go to

college, to be a marine biologist, get married. . ." His voice choked then trailed off.

"Marion, do you believe in God?" Jill's soothing voice asked.

The dispatcher nodded jerkily.

"Ask God to be with you and Kelsey, and I'll pray too. . ."

King beat a retreat, leaving them to their God talk. He never would have taken Marion for a Christian, not with his drinking problem and smart mouth, but as he walked out into the spring sun, King knew he'd been so wrapped up in himself and his pain that he'd missed the signs of a man in trouble. A niggle of guilt touched him. Everyone needed at least one friend to lean on when it got tough. Without Sam he'd probably be dead in the back of some Texas Honky Tonk. Sam never seemed to miss the signs of impending trouble.

Jill didn't either. She'd seen something and reached out. Maybe she wasn't like some of those Holy Rollers that came around after he'd gotten back from Iraq. All they'd wanted was the lowdown on what had happened to Carol, leave a casserole, and then disappear. The food hadn't even been that great.

No, this one was different—and dangerously so.

He waited patiently in his truck until Jill made a flustered appearance, blowing out of the office door like the devil was after her. She stood in the spring sunlight, letting her glasses adjust to the sudden brightness, and looked around wildly as though forgetting why she had been rushing. King grinned, taking the moment to admire the little lady. She was put together rather nice. He particularly like the way the sun brought out the red in her hair, as though she wore her own little halo of sunshine.

Those velvet brown eyes lit on him in the UPS truck and she grimaced. She hurried down the steps and climbed aboard her own truck. The smile stuck in place for no good reason, even after her truck inched forward. Jamming his truck into drive, he growled to himself. How did she always get him grinning like a goof? Just being around her pierced years of carefully cultivated gruffness designed to keep people and emotions at a distance. Funny as this was, he didn't want her to know that man. Already shame plagued him about the way they'd met. No, she made him want to find that other man, the person before the bitterness overwhelmed him. He shook his head. *You're being a fool. That someone is long gone. She had it right in the first place. King Snake describes you perfectly. Best remember why you're here and why you're alone.*

***

The pair of UPS trucks pulled out of the yard under Sam's watchful eye. He let the blinds drop into place, smoothing them down as his mind wandered. He had prayed about sending Jill with King. Was it the right decision? How many times had he asked God to send someone who could pull King from where he wallowed in a well of hate and anger? Like an answer to prayer, here came Jill. As a recruiter, he met just about every woman that came through Sea2Sea. But this lady from Texas seemed to have something extra. That something special that he knew instinctively King needed. She had just the right mix of sweet and steel with an air of injured vulnerability few men could resist.

He shook his head and set back to work, a9lways amazed at the working of the Holy Spirit and how two people from Texas had to come to Indiana to meet up and get their lives right.

CHAPTER NINE

Miles unfolded like an uncut ribbon, sliding off the spool with the mile markers. Despite the late start, King was confident his five hundred mile goal could be reached. Jill didn't mind. Freedom tasted honey sweet. She'd always dreamed of traveling, but marriage, family, and money always seemed to be in the way. No more. Even if the circumstances that forced her leaving everything behind weren't that great, she would take advantage of it and see the U.S.

As though anticipating her need to see beauty, the artist's palate of nut brown farmlands with their spears of new growth passed like the blurred colors of a priceless Monet. She took a deep breath of the breeze as it whipped through the side window, then grimaced when she hit a bump. The well sprung seat, plainly designed for someone much taller and heavier, tried to eject her through the ceiling—again.

The jolt caused her foot to slip off the gas pedal and the whole trucked rocked. She flushed. Daddy would have chewed her raw if he could see her now. Though the truck shifted smooth as any car, to the world she looked like a novice driver on a standard. The vehicles sharing Interstate 55 sped up and gave her plenty of room, leaving her staring at the back of King's class A truck, one much bigger than her own.

She now understood why the dispatcher had hinted that making the run with someone who knew the ins and outs of this job would be a good thing. She'd been so flustered about actually driving off with her first load, she'd almost cruised by the affiliate gas station to fill up where the Sea2Sea drivers got discounted fuel. Then, after assuring King she was on top of things, she nearly missed following the other brown truck onto the entrance for the interstate.

On a good note, the cool, spring day made perfect driving conditions—even in an unairconditioned box, even with the spine jarring, teeth rattling, mind numbing bouncing. Her phone beeped and she frowned at where it sat on top of her bag in the aisle beside her. The seventh time since leaving the yard. She didn't dare check it, not without a good bit of the type of weaving that could draw the eye of a police cruiser. Besides, she knew without looking it was from Stu. He evidently put himself on a schedule and had texted every half hour.

She gritted her teeth and sighed as the lights of a passing diner whizzed past. Would this guy ever stop? For 150 miles he had driven like a robot, dead straight, needle stuck at 60 mph. A sudden cold sweat trickled down her shoulder blades as she thought about the texts. What if it wasn't Stu? What if Shawn needed to talk to her? What if he'd been in an accident and it was the hospital? She kept her eyes glued to the road. Reality blurred into daymares.

It could be Stacy. Had her daughter finally tracked down her number? Maybe threatened it out of Shawn? She reached for her phone, unable to stand not knowing a minute longer. A bump jarred the seat, sending her towards the ceiling once more. The phone tumbled to the ground on the walk in side, but not before she saw the hippie driver's smug face in the box next to the number.

She relaxed and steadied the truck. What was it with him anyway? She'd gone to lunch with him. Once. So he had helped her. Did he have to text every few seconds to see if she was alright?

She sifted through the information he had thrown at her during his non-stop monologue. Honestly, she tried to listen to everything, but he flitted from topic to topic like a man with a bad case of ADHD. Most of his information made no sense or was colored with opinion and criticisms. Married three times, had a 12 year-old-boy with the last wife with whom he still technically lived when not on the road. Standard stuff for a truck driver, she supposed. The phone beeped again.

Should she signal King she wanted a break? He seemed adamant about making three hundred miles and that mark fast approached. 'I don't stop 'till my truck's empty' he'd said. The phone beeped again. She shrugged. *Oh well.*

At long last, in Springfield, Illinois, King turned off the interstate and eased into a fuel at a Pilot truck stop. Jill parked behind him and finally snatched her phone from the floor. Quickly she scrolled through, most from Stu with a single call from King. With a sigh, she turned to get out of the truck and screamed as she came face to face with the tall cowboy on the other side of the glass.

She slid open the door. "You scared me."

"Why didn't you answer your phone?"

She blushed, but refused to look away from his probing eyes. For some reason she was reluctant to mention the texts from Stu. "I couldn't reach it mostly and the driver's manual said not to—"

"Don't quote the manual to me—I helped write the thang."

She waved a hand. "Yeah, but—"

She squeaked again when he leaned forward and surveyed the dash. "You need a Blue tooth or something. You can't run with someone if you can't communicate."

"Uh, okay?"

He leaned back and studied the truck with practiced eyes. "What's going on back here, anyway?"

"What do you mean?"

King shook his head as though she were a foreigner trying to understand Texan. "You're jerkin' all over the place. I thought for sure a couple times you were headed for the rails."

"Well, the seat keeps jumping around like it a bucking bull. I'm about black and blue from head to derriere." She jutted her chin out at him to try to make him understand it wasn't due to her awful driving or because she was a woman. He seemed to like to blame things on that.

He just gave her an odd look and reached up towards her chair.

With a jerk her seat dropped towards the floor. "Is that about right?" She nodded. He fiddled with the seat again.

She tried to bounce, but it stayed locked in place. "Wow, that will be so much better. Thanks."

He grunted. "You have to lock the thing down or you'll be jumping all over." He turned and walked back to his truck to begin fueling.

Jill frowned at his retreating back. "That's what I said." He continued like he hadn't heard. *Sometimes he's so grumpy.* But then there were other times, like laughing together at the hotel, that a connection seemed to snap between them. She had to admit to herself, she liked this man, and if she really thought about it, it wasn't just because they'd been thrown together. She didn't seemed to feel that way about any of the other men she'd met over the last few days. She shook the thoughts from her head. This sort of thing was not what she needed right now. Romantic entanglements did not mesh with running for your life or keeping a low profile.

Her phone rang. "Hello?"

"Hi, Jill. Stu. How's your first load treating you?"

"Great." So far it had been a nightmare, but things were going smoothly now. Besides, she wasn't one to air her troubles just to hear herself whine. She watched as King went in to pay for his fuel.

"That's great. Just remember, if you have any questions, give me a call. If you need a ride somewhere and I'm within a couple hundred miles, I'll come get you, don't you worry."

"Uh, thanks, Stu. I have to go now, King's moving his truck and I'm next."

"King? You're running with King?"

Why's he so uptight? The cowboy's name seemed to make him angry, catching her off her guard.

"Yes, he took that other UPS going to Phoenix."

"Well, someone must be playing favorites, then. I asked for that load."

"I thought you were tow-away." *Like King*.

"I am, but it looked like a good load. We could have been traveling together, getting to know each other better."

Alarm bells dinged in the back of her brain, but the vacated fuel aisle caught her attention.

Last thing she wanted was to slow her companion down again. "Sorry, Stu, I have to go, I don't want to hold up the line."

"Well, okay then, you just be careful around King, Jill. Like I said before, he has a reputation for being unpredictable. One time—" *Why so insistent on warning me about King?*

"Okay then, bye bye." Clicking her phone closed, she tossed it into her bag and pulled into the fuel aisle, not sure if she wanted to talk to Stu again. She couldn't tell if it was because she didn't want to encourage him, or that she didn't like the way he talked about King. The cowboy's temper seemed mercurial, true, but she couldn't quite pin unpredictable on him. But she would be careful. She knew exactly how fast a person could change.

CHAPTER TEN

Her belly rumbled, protesting her small snack of sunflower seeds. It seemed like a good idea at the time, something she could grab and go while King stood by the door watching, but eating them had proved near impossible as she drove, with the breeze from the window pushing more shells back into the cab than she threw out the window. Finally, she chucked them all out for birds to enjoy.

She'd kept her phone handy, just in case her fearless leader called to let her know it was to stop and eat, but once again the only texts came from Stu. Midnight approached. Despite her hunger, reluctance to pester the other driver about stopping kept her going. She needed to prove she could hang with the big dogs.

Taking a deep breath, she choked on the diesel fumes. Despite the late hour, big rigs packed the parking lot in perfectly aligned rows. King found one of the last open spots, then directed her to pull in behind him. Together the two trucks equaled the length of a nearby 53 footer. Once she'd parked, he turned and headed back toward the truck stop without a word. By the time she jumped out of the truck, even the greasy spoon across the street looked like a good place to hunt up some food. King didn't even glance at the flashing yellow sign. *No wonder he's so skinny.*

While waiting in line to pay for fuel, a tantalizing smell wafted by. She nearly gave up her place in the busy checkout line to find something more substantial than sunflower seeds. Her stomach rumbled again, this time loudly enough to turn several heads.

King raised an eyebrow up into his hat brim. "Hungry?"

She nodded.

King looked around. "Normally I would advise against eating at a truck stop, the food's as nasty as it's rumored to be, but they have a sandwich shop here too. Why don't you get something?"

She gritted her teeth, determined to eat when he did. "Don't you eat?"

He looked at her in surprise. "Of course. I keep a cooler that plugs into the truck. I keep it stocked–carrot sticks, cauliflower, apples. That sort of thing."

She stared at him, anger building. All the time she thought he'd been driving, he'd been eating, while here she was at the brink of starvation. Her stomach rumbled again. She ducked her head in embarrassment, but couldn't stop the humor of the situation from making her smile. Couldn't blame her hunger on him, she should have asked him about eating earlier. She just needed to ask more questions, that was all, even if it meant driving him crazy. She paid for her fuel and went to get a sandwich.

***

King shook his head as he caught a whisper of Jill's quiet chuckling. *Woman's always laughing about something or other. She didn't even take starving herself seriously.* Guilt prodded his conscience as he thought about her standing here in line, her stomach rumbling, stubborn jaw thrust out, refusing to eat unless he did. The cauliflower he'd had a few miles back sat like a lump in his stomach as well. *Crazy lady, throws a kink in everything, even digestion.* He sighed and headed to the sandwich shop. *Might as well get dinner.* A warm roast beef sandwich might help those veggies settle.

***

An awkward silence reigned as Jill tried to think of something to say that wouldn't upset her companion. He'd grabbed a sandwich and sat at her booth, but he never said a word. She stifled a yawn, pushing at the remains of her sandwich. King sat across from her, munching through his meal with the single mindedness that belonged to the realm of men and teenagers.

She racked her brain for a conversation starter, but exhaustion fuzzed her thinking. If talking religion got under his skin then she definitely couldn't try politics. Any question about the past was delicate. Both hers and his.

"You married?" She gulped down a bite as cold blue eyes meant hers. *Where'd that come from?*

"I live in my truck, Jill. I don't keep a wife in the jockey box."

She dropped her eyes to the wrapper. "Oh, guess not." The silence between them became even more awkward. "Sorry, I didn't mean to pry. Just trying to make conversation."

He regarded her for a long moment before shrugging. "I think you'll find most of the guys at Sea2Sea aren't married, or aren't going to be for much longer, some just got married, for a multiple time. Truck driving is hard on marriages, so it's best if you just stick to the job or the weather."

Jill pulled a wilted piece of lettuce out of her sandwich and grimaced. "Or food?"

He nodded solemnly. "Food is usually safe."

She poked at the green lump. "So is this why you don't eat at truck stops?"

"I've had a few bouts with food poisoning over the years. Most times from places little better than this."

"Don't you ever miss a home cooked meal? I already miss them and this is my first day on the road."

He shrugged. "You get used to it. Carol—" Jill's head jerked up, and caught his slight nod, "my ex-wife, she wasn't much of a cook anyways. We ate out a lot."

Jill mulled this tidbit of information over in her head. She studied his face. Crows feet from hours of squinting into the sun, mouth mostly hidden. It was a visage that showed a deep sadness. His eyes focused on the far wall. He pushed away his half eaten sandwich as though it were distasteful and stood. "Are you done? We should turn in so we can get an early start tomorrow." His voice had turned from friendly to a growl in the pause.

"Sure." *Was it Carol that made him so mad at*

the world? She didn't dare ask. His long strides already carried him towards the exit. She wrapped the remainder of her meal in the wrapper and followed.

***

"So where do we sleep?" Jill asked on a puff as she jogged beside the long-legged cowboy.

"What do you mean?"

She blushed, realizing that question could be taken wrong. "I mean, umm. . ."

In the parking lot lights she saw his teeth flash in a smile, as though her discomfort amused him. "You have two options. The shelf in the truck."

She studied at the brown box. The late night air made her fingers tingle with the cold. Turning her mood sour. Not too difficult to imagine how the floor would feel after a day of the jouncing in the crazy killer seat. She looked hopefully at King. Surely there was a better option.

He pointed across the street. "There's also the motel."

The superior tone of his words indicated he

wouldn't be staying there.

"Where are you sleeping?"

"The truck."

"Really?"

He blew out a breath as though annoyed, but explained anyway. "Drive-aways have to watch every penny or they end up short on the back end. Plus bed bugs are real."

She shuddered. "So you sleep in the truck."

He tipped his hat with a nod. "That would be right. Good night."

He left her standing in the semi-light, trying to figure out what to do. Honestly, she didn't know where she would find the energy to walk across the street.

"But what about a shower?" She called after him..

He paused the in the door of his truck and pointed back the way they'd come. "Truck stop. Five bucks."

"Yikes."

The door on his truck slid shut with a muffled

bang and a note of finality. Okay then. She faced the travel center and ran her tongue over her teeth. She was tired, but. . .with a sigh she headed back to get her toiletries. She'd hurry. One day on the road would not turn her into a caricature of a truck driver.

CHAPTER ELEVEN

Jill punched her pillow and twisted in her sleeping bag, trying to get comfortable. Two minutes later her phone beeped the seven o'clock alarm. She groaned and sat up, rubbing her shoulder. The narrow shelf in the back of the UPS truck built for holding packages made her miss a mattress.

She slid the phone open at another beep.

Stu: Are you rolling yet this morning?

Right on the hour—didn't that guy ever sleep?

Beep

Shawn: Good morning, Mom. Have a good day on the road.

She rolled over, feet hitting the cold metal

floor with a thump. King would be itchin' to go.

Only the second day and she felt like she was a piece of asphalt instead of the one driving on it. She ran a brush through her hair, didn't want to scare her driving partner again, and swished her mouth with some water. She jumped into the driver's seat and looked over at the other truck. The cowboy sat in the front seat as though he'd been there for hours, just waiting for her to wake. He touched his hat. She resisted the urge to stick out her tongue. His mustache twitched as though he knew exactly the thoughts going through her head. His brown truck rumbled to life.

Feeling the sudden call of nature, she held up a finger, grabbed her bag and hurried through the oil scented air to the truck stop to take care of her morning business.

A few minutes later she hustled from the restrooms and spied King at the coffee counter. Good. He wasn't revving the truck waiting for her. He took a cup from the Caribou Coffee attendant and turned with his steaming cup of joe.

She nearly melted. "That smells wonderful."

He stepped aside so she could order."Could I have a Small Hot Dark Chocolate Ho Ho Mint Mocha?"

The attendant wrote her order. "Whipped cream?"

"As much as it will hold."

"Lite?"

Did she look like she took it light? "No. The real stuff, please."

In three minutes she breathed in the minty aroma and risked a tiny sip of the hot liquid. Feeling King's eyes she looked up and smiled. "Just what I needed. This will definitely hit the spot."

"A ho ho mint--" He frowned as he stumbled.

"Dark chocolate Ho Ho mint mocha. Ever had one?"

He shook his head.

"You should try it. The syrup and candy canes give it that extra boost."

He covered his own mug like she would try to add something on the sly.

She peered at the brown liquid. "What do you have?"

He pulled it away. "Coffee."

"Just coffee?"

He nodded.

"Black?"

Another nod.

"I should have known."

"What does that mean?"

"I don't know. You just seem like the type of person to take it straight up. Kind of gruff. I bet when you get the chance to make a pot the mugs run away screaming it's so stout."

His mustache twitched. "Maybe." She liked it when he smiled. It changed his whole face. He seemed younger than she originally thought.

He looked towards the trucks, bringing her mind back to business.

"Ready?"

"Sure, where to today?"

He opened a ratty atlas and thumped his finger on their position. "It's 44 West from here on." He flipped a few pages. "How's Oklahoma sound?"

Did he honestly want her opinion? "Sounds great."

She studied the man as he turned back to his map, from the tall hat shadowing the salt and pepper mustache, to his crazily adorned boots that screamed cowboy. Although raised in Indiana, she'd lived long enough in Texas to meet all sorts of men. From the polished city slickers of Dallas to the crease-faced rodeo chasers with dirt from a thousand arenas beat into every pore. Overall, she liked the men the big state bred. She shivered and pulled her sweater closer. Coming back North, people seemed colder somehow. Pushier.

This man seemed to stand out above all the others. He was so full of contradictions. Gruff, but helpful. Taking charge, then asking her opinion. Despite that, she already felt comfortable around him. He seemed more real about his true self (as crusty as that was) and had no interest in putting on a false front. She despised that.

Besides, she liked the gentleness of the South.

The hat tippin' and the ma'ams. It gave her a powerful, feminine feeling. Like she was the belle of the ball with the power of Scarlet O'Hara. Who'd have thought she find it in Indiana? King pulled it off well too, the small acts of chivalry seemed so natural she knew he'd grown up opening doors and minding his manners around a woman that loved him enough to teach him how a lady liked to be treated. What turns a man so sour that people looked at him cross-eyed? Just thinking about her own past—dare she ask?

King looked up as though feeling her eyes. "Everything alright?"

She nodded. "Sure. Why?"

"Yer phone's been going off every 30 seconds or so for a while now. You kinda zoned out."

Staring at him at taken her off into lala land. She looked at her phone. "Just Stu—again."

Eyebrows rose as the blue eyes took their turn to study her. "Stu? From work?"

She flashed him the phone. "I don't know why he feels the need to keep up with me. He texts all the time."

The man stayed silent, eyes intent on his coffee while the air grew thick with censor. Without another word he started towards the door. Disapproval radiated from the stiff set of his shoulders and sharp click of his boots.

She jogged after him, trying to keep the whipped cream of her coffee from slopping out. How come it seemed she was always chasing him down. Shouldn't it be the other way around? She almost stopped when the thought crossed her mind. *Where did that come from?* No one needed to be chasing anyone. She was on this job for one reason. To keep moving.

Still, something she said had made him angry, and she was determined to find out what it was. She touched his arm. "Did I say something wrong?" Of course, she hadn't, but it didn't hurt to ask.

He shrugged. "Nothing. None of my business."

Now she knew and she couldn't believe it. He thought she's 'hooked up' with Stu! "Now look here. It's not like that."

He raised a hand, cutting her off in mid-sentence. "Like I said. None of my business what you do."

Jill stared after him. Did he honestly think she'd started something with another driver? She'd only just met the other man. Matter of fact, she'd only just met either of them and here he thought he could judge her. These men. One spent his time warning her away from the other, the other thinking – she didn't know what. Anger burned low in her gut and she chased after the long legged cowboy.

"Wait a minute. I don't want any misunderstandings between us. I don't know what I've done to make Stu think he needs to text every half hour, even during the night, but—"

He sighed. "Look, Lady—"

Oh lady was it now?

"Women—and men—come and go through our company, lots of them get together now and again. I'd just rather not know about everyone else's truck. Just keep me out of the loop okay. You keep yours. I keep mine."

"My what?"

"Baggage, secrets. Whatever, this ain't a T.V. show, we don't have to air dirty laundry to each other."

"Dirty laundry? There isn't any dirty laundry? Besides, there's something about that guy that gives me the creeps and I don't know why I'm explaining myself to you at all. Do you go around thinking bad of everyone?"

He stared at her silently for a moment. "Why are you angry?"

"I'm not angry."

"You're shouting."

"I'm not—" She lowered her voice and took a deep breath. "I just don't like being judged because some guy took it on himself to text me. As though you were looking for something. . ." She let her voice trail off, surprised at how much it hurt to think that he didn't like her. She took a step away, realizing that she'd been leaning into his space. "I'm sorry about that." She forced a smile. It felt stiff, but then she relaxed as he didn't respond one way or the other. Instead, he watched her as though bemused. "I'm ready now."

"Feeling better?"

She nodded. "Sorry. I guess he's been driving me nuts."

"Why don't you tell him to stop then?"

"I think I will. Thanks."

He tipped his hat and opened the door to his truck without another word.

CHAPTER TWELVE

The phone rang as she jumped into the truck. Thinking it might be Stu again she grabbed it, and flipped it open. "Stu, you need to quit calling me–"

"Mom?"

Her heart stuttered and stopped. The voice whispered in her ear from the past, so loved. So feared. Not Shawn. No, not the child who stood by her through it all. The speaker was the other offspring, the one she prayed for daily. She never could tell if she asked for peace or for forgetfulness.

The husky voice haunted her dreams. The last thing she'd heard as death stalked through the smoke of her burning home. Even now she could feel the thick hand around her chest, replacing the air with burning.

The bitter stench of her flaming couch filled her nostrils again. She tried to breath deep and looked around, grounding herself. She focused on the garish yellow and green sign of the truck stop, willing away the panic. The burning house and pain wasn't here.

"Mom?" The voice repeated "I gotta to talk to you. I've tried to write, but they come back. Mom? You there? I know why you don't want to talk to me, I understand. But we gotta talk."

How could Shawn do this to her? She'd changed her number at least two, no three, times. The the only way Stacy could have found her was through her brother.

"Are you there? Please—"

Jill slid the phone shut, closed her eyes and tried breathing. Her ribs ached from holding her breath. Her heart, now deciding it could beat, galloped uncontrollably in her chest. She sat gasping in the seat, watching the trucks come and go, transported back in time with the sound of Stacy's voice ringing in her ears.

***

"This time you've gone and done it, Mom."

Jill had just walked through the door from work, keys and purse still dangling from her hand, the only things on her mind something to eat, a hot bath, and bed. Stacy had other plans, cornering her in the narrow kitchen. She leaned in close, wide eyed and yelling.

Stacy knew exactly when to choose her battles. "Why did you tell them it was me? I didn't even do it. Now they've arrested Smokey and he's mad at me. All because you went to the police over a few measly checks."

Jill struggled to recall the incident that had her daughter so incensed. She barely remembered calling the police after the missing checks began bouncing at the bank. She'd told the police that she didn't know who could have gotten them. Maybe her ex, Chuck, found some before she'd thrown him out to go live with his mistress. Staring at Stacy's livid face, she realized that it wasn't the ex. Somehow it had something to do with her daughter.

"You? You gave Smokey my checks?" She asked despite the evidence of the answer before her. Then it dawned on her. She had unwittingly gotten her daughter involved with the police and though just 20, the kid already had a rap sheet, drugs, prostitution – now this. "Why, Stacy? I don't have any money, *you* of all people should know that."

But her daughter didn't answer. She paced the tiny kitchen, banging her hands on the counter as she yelled the question over and over. "Why'd you turn me in? Why? Why? Why?" The question turned into a chant. Jill narrowed her eyes, recognizing the jerky movements, the wild eyes as the burn of drugs.

Still she tried to reason with her. "I didn't turn *you* in, Honey. I reported to the police about someone writing bad checks on my account."

Jill turned to hang her keys on the hook, never seeing the first blow. She fell against the dining table. Face exploding with pain. Stacy had the large hands of her father–and they hurt just as bad. She'd also learned just how to hit her just like he did, she watched enough of their fights. Jill put a hand to her cheek, it came away crimson from where the skin had split on her cheek bone. She cried out as another fist slid across her face, breaking her nose.

The world spun, the linoleum reached up and grabbed her, yanking her to the floor and cracking against her temple. The dirt caked under the cabinets mingled with old dog hair caught her eye. *I'll have to clean that.* The kick that broke two ribs sent her rolling into the dining room.

Stacy shrieked, kicking at her prone body to punctuate each word. "I didn't do it. They arrested Smokey this morning."

Jill fought to focus through the blood clouding her vision. Her thoughts seemed fuzzy—faraway. She struggled for words. "You gave my checks to your drug dealing boyfriend? Why? How?"

Stacy was beyond answering, she continued kicking and hitting until everything went black. The next thing she remembered was crawling out the back door as the house filled with smoke, Teyo helping her and then the police and the ambulance. Stacy spewing hate.

***

King banged on the door. "Jill, we going anywhere today?" He'd been idling at the exit for five minutes, waiting for her to pull in behind him. Her little brown truck never moved. This woman couldn't keep on track for anything. Probably on the phone *with Stu.* The door slid open. Angry words froze on his lips. He took in her chalk white pallor, the chocolate eyes glazed through her driving glasses, unseeing and haunted with memories.

Like a beaten dog, she cringed away from him as though afraid he'd hit her. Instantly he took a step back, giving her room. He'd never laid a hand on a woman in anger, but by her reaction he could tell this lady had been man handled at some point. He cautiously reached for the nearest hand and clasped it in his own. It was so small, cold and trembling. He wrapped his own fingers around it, trying to will his warmth into her.

He'd seen this many times before over in Iraq, experienced it a few times himself. That overwhelming numbness that crept up and overtook a body when everything was just too much. "Hey there. You with me?" He eased into his words, talking as though she were a skittish filly.

She shuddered and finally took a deep breath. Her eyes cleared of the vagueness, but not of the tears. "Oh. Hi. I'm sorry." She blinked, focusing on the truck stop and the present.

He chafed the tiny hand, trying to warm it. "Are you okay?"

Another stuttering breath. "Oh, sure. Why are you here? I thought we were leaving?"

He studied her for a moment. "I've been waiting at the exit. You never came."

She tried to smile. "I'm really sorry, an unexpected phone call, that's all."

Anger coursed through him. "Stu again?" He'd yank that long hair hippie's head off his shoulders. What gave him the right to pester someone to tears?

"Oh, no, not him." As though conscious of her

hand in his she slowly extricated her fingers. He stared at his hand as it betrayed him by missing the feel of her fingers in his. "Thank-you for waiting for me."

"I'm not gonna leave you." He searched his brain for something to put her at her ease. "We're partners, right?"

She grinned, the light in her eyes returning. Shining through unshed tears. "Right."

King straightened. "You okay to drive? You don't have them panic attacks on the road do you?"

"Panic attacks?" She rolled the word around on her tongue, as though it were a familiar taste that couldn't be placed. "Well, it's been awhile. I haven't had one since. . ." Her voice trailed off. "But I'm okay, really, just an expected call." She looked him square in the face and gave him that smile he recognized as mere bravado. "But you know I don't answer the phone while I'm on the road so we'll have none of that."

He nodded. She seemed back to normal. The tears gone, breathing regular. "Okay then. Tell me if you have to pull over then."

"I'm fine. Thanks."

He didn't believe that she was okay, not for one minute, but he wasn't going to go digging when the other person obviously didn't want to talk. He'd watch her though, these panic attacks struck at the oddest times and might be dangerous if she didn't know where she was or where she was going.

CHAPTER THIRTEEN

It was always like this after contact with Stacy. Thoughts running wild, regrets, wishing for do overs that just didn't happen. The same question beat at her over and over. *Where did I go wrong?* She'd wanted so much to be friends with her firstborn. Oh, such naive dreams of princess parties and lace dresses. A child she could dress up and show off to the parents who disapproved of her first husband. It hadn't taken her long to figure out why either. Maybe she'd tried too hard to hide the issues in her marriage from Stacy. It had made Jill furtive and silent. Her daughter took that as a signal to run roughshod over her mother, using fists like her husband.

From the get go she'd fought Jill with cruel biting words from the time she first talked. After the second year there were no bows or dresses, she wanted short hair and pants. She didn't want dolls, and refused to participate in art or dance. Jill tried activity after activity to try to catch her daughter's attention, but she had her own agenda from early on, and it had nothing to do with anyone else's. Least of all her abused mother's.

The thought of a second child terrified her. In the wee hours of the night, before Shawn moved, she contemplated going to a clinic. She hated herself thinking it, knowing that even if God could forgive her, she'd never forgive herself. Then her boy arrived, so sweet and full of life. He played quietly on his own while Stacy stormed around the house, and she began to wonder if it wasn't just that she was an awful mother.

As teenagers their differences became even more pronounced. Shawn joined the science and debate teams. Stacy started skipping school and finally dropped out to hang out with a bad crowd. Shawn tried to make up for everything by being the perfect son-finally leaving for an engineering job in Los Angeles. It was hard not to compare them, to love them for their own good qualities, but it became harder and harder to see them in her daughter.

Pulling onto the interstate, she relaxed into her seat. Praying for peace. Praying for invisibility. Praying that her daughter never found her. After 30 minutes of begging God to keep her safe she realized all she needed to do was claim the promise that He heard all the pleas of her heart. Her thoughts turned more pleasant immediately. They drifted to the gruff cowboy with an unexpected kind side. The warmth and gentleness of his hands had surprised her and she smiled a little when she thought of the long fingers completely engulfing hers. How she'd wanted to stay like that forever. Feeling safe and warm. Then she frowned. He evidently knew about panic attacks. Where had that come from?

For the few miles she occupied herself with

thoughts of the taciturn man, ruminating over Stu's warnings about him. He had yelled at Sam, but it lacked the bite a truly angry man used. The recruiter obviously had a respect and liking for the tall driver. And what about the concern he showed for her? None of it seemed to fit into what Stu hinted was a dangerous man.

To top it all off, she liked him and the way he treated her. He opened doors, touched his hat—that was just too cute, and the more he talked to her, the more he seemed to open up. She sighed. Maybe she'd been alone too long and was grasping at straws, but she definitely didn't feel this way about Stu. But why would she meet someone she was interested in now? When her life was turmoil and finding her God intended partner had to be the last thing on her mind?

These thoughts kept her brain from focusing on the gathering storm in her heart. Every time she glanced at her phone she jerked her eyes back to the road. Refusing to think that Stacy actually might be able to find her and that God had a plan for sending this tall cowboy into her life.

***

The flat plains of west Texas never looked so good. Although the truck did the moving, Jill felt as though she'd run a marathon and limped across the finish line in last place. Her muscles groaned, bruised from the constant jarring. She rolled her eyes, trying to get rid of the sand feeling and rubbing only made it worse. A look in the review mirror showed them to be red and angry looking. But—she'd made it. 675 miles, give or take, a long stretch, but still legal according to King. There had only been one stop, somewhere in western Oklahoma where she changed her phone number, then pushing on. If King's intent was to break her in easy—she'd hate to see hard.

A shower went a long way to making her feel human again. She settled herself in the truck, her hunger pains eased with a cardboard-tasting microwave burrito from the stop, then snuggled down into her sleeping bag and called Shawn. Her anger, simmering all day in the Texas heat, finally flared.

He answered on the first ring. "Hi, Mom."

Was it just her, or did those two words sound guilty? She'd texted him earlier with her new number, and he ought to know why she changed it. She cut straight to the issue. "Why did you tell her?"

The silence at the other end lasted longer than usual. Her son often took time to think before speaking, turning the words over and over in his head. Sometimes for days. On a good day she thought it a good sign, the mark of deliberate mind that wouldn't make split second, hair brained decisions like she did. Today it wore on her. "Shawn?"

"She needs to talk to you, Mom."

She gritted her teeth. He'd only been 15 at the time of the attack and his big sister held a special place in his heart. Of course he would want to heal the breech and bring his family back together. In her own mind she understood why. But he hadn't even been home at the time. He just didn't understand. He hadn't seen the anger and viciousness in her face. Even though Stacy surely loved her brother, Jill didn't know if it would have stopped her from hurting him that day as well. And she was so glad she hadn't had to find out.

She tried to explain. "Can't you understand why I don't want to talk to her? She called me and threatened me already."

"She threatened you?"

"Yes, told me she wanted to find me. Why would you do that? Give her the means to get in touch with me?"

Silence. Her temper flared. "Answer me now, Shawn Elliot."

His sigh whispered through the phone. "I've been in touch with her for years, Mom."

"You what?"

"And when she said she wanted to talk to you, to come clean, I gave her your number."

She couldn't keep the sarcasm out her her voice. "And you believed her? Why?"

"She's been in prison ten years—"

"Yes, for the attempted murder *of her mother.*"

"—she's changed."

"And you're willing to bet my life on that?"

Silence.

"Are you?"

"I have all the letters she's ever written to me. She *has* changed. I've seen it."

"Before or after the years added for attacking a prison guard."

"Mom, just listen—"

"No, you listen. You have no right to make those kinds of decisions for me. To give someone who tried to kill me my number—you didn't even speak to me about it first. You could have told me about the letters and talking to her in prison, but you didn't, it came out of the blue. And let me tell you, I don't want to talk to her. It wasn't you she pounded into the floor and kicked till she broke ribs. You weren't there when she lit the house on fire around me and stood laughing outside while it burned— with me in it. So don't you presume to tell me I need to listen to you."

"Mom, where's your forgiveness? You're always talking about moving on, following God's leading in your life." Shawn's gentle voice reached through the phone, but no way was she going to let this little bit of treachery pass. Her little boy thought he was all grown up now, making these decisions like she'd gone senile. She swallowed at the stinging in her throat.

How could he betray her like this? *She* wasn't forgiving? "Just because I don't want to see her, doesn't mean I haven't forgiven her." Hadn't she asked the judge for leniency? Hadn't she refused to testify? Not like they needed her anyway. The evidence had been there. Stacy admitted to everything. Including trying to kill her mother.

"You haven't." His voice rang with finality. "It's eating at you. You hide behind the facade that you're getting a new job and going on the road because you can, that God's leading—but Mom, you won't even talk about her. You haven't mentioned her name since the trial. You preach God's love to everyone—but you don't embrace it yourself."

Jill fumbled the phone. Her son was no orator —he wrote and expressed himself well when he wanted to, but that was maybe the most words she'd heard out of him all strung together in a year. What the niggling suspicion in the back of her had that he had nailed the truth of the matter on the head hurt the most.

Her breath came out in a whoosh. "That's not fair."

"Maybe."

Her anger vented—she had nothing left. Changing the subject seemed trivial, but she definitely didn't want to talk about this any longer. "I love you, Shawn. I'll call you later."

He paused, as though he had more to say. Unspoken words seared the cell frequencies, but all that came through were the simple words they ended every phone call with. "Love you too. Be careful out there."

"I will."

Closing the phone, she stood and stared out the front window at the lines of trucks. She climbed out of the sleeping bag and shrugged into her coat. Maybe a walk would help clear her mind.

The engines rumbled like purring lions as she weaved her way back towards the lights of the truck stop. Most of the front curtains were closed tight, some were lit by the luminescent glow of electronics She stood outside the doors of the travel center, not wanting to enter, but longing for that tiny touch of humanity that kept the darkness at bay. The place still bustled, even at this time of night. She just wanted some place quiet that wasn't the box of her truck.

"Jill?" King's voice rolled over her like the sound of the engines she'd just passed. He leaned against a brick pillar, a cup of joe sending tendrils of steam into the chilly night.

She squinted against the light. "Are you following me?"

His head straightened and he lifted the cup. "I was here first, Ma'am."

She felt his eyes studying her, judging her. Her skin itched, like it wanted to crawl away. She sighed. "I'm sorry. It's just been a tough couple of days. I'm just trying to get some air and it seems like there isn't any place that isn't reeking of diesel or full of people."

"This *is* a truck stop."

"So it is."

"Stu been bothering you again?" He grimaced at the question, as though it sprang unbidden from his mouth.

She shook her head, hiding the little smile his reaction caused. "No. I changed my number this afternoon."

"That might explain it."

"What?"

"Why you didn't answer again."

She palmed her brow. While calling Shawn, her parents and sisters, she'd forgotten about the man driving the truck in front of her and what he'd said about keeping the lines of communication open. "I'm sorry."

He shrugged. "No need to keep apologizing. We made it." Drinking down the last of his coffee, he threw the cup into a trash bin and straightened. "I'm headed in before the lot lizards get to work."

"Lot lizards?"

He blinked then motioned towards the trucks. "The ladies. Don't worry though, they don't usually bother the UPS trucks."

She looked around, realizing belatedly that a walk this time of night might not be in her best interest. "Can I walk with you?"

"Suit yourself."

She fell in beside him, the silence stretched, and despite his kindness and seemingly never ending patience, longer it went on the more she felt she needed to explain herself to this man. He must think her a number one kook from the looney bin. "I know you must think me a few cards short of a full deck, but everything just seems to be happening at once. Thanks–" For what? Not going on a tirade because she'd over slept? Because she couldn't get it in her head to keep in touch with her partner? Her back bent in defeat. "Just thanks."

He lifted his shoulders as though her words

made him uncomfortable. "It's no problem. You haven't slowed me down or anything."

She hid a smile. Hadn't slowed him down had she? She stopped by the door of the truck. "Well, I'm glad you took the load. I know you didn't want to—Sam pulling in some favors and all. Despite what people say about you, you've been a great blessing to me."

"People? Like Stu?"

She nodded. "He didn't have a whole lot of nice to say." She held up her hands. "Don't worry, I try not to believe every bad thing I hear about someone before I get to know them."

He laughed, reminding her she liked the sound of it. "That's good to know." He sobered suddenly. "But you should listen to people." His eyes looked across the desert. "Most rumors have a bit of truth in them." Was he threatening her? Just the thought that this man that she didn't even know might be the type of person to turn on her as well caused the tears to come unbidden. She sniffed and wiped at them, trying to hide it.

He glanced down at her, as though jerked from where ever his mind wandered. "Jill?"

She waved a hand. "Never mind me." All she needed was him of accusing her of trying to air her dirty laundry again. "Long day. I'm tired. Goodnight." She turned and fumbled with the keys to her truck.

"Truck driving's tough." He offered. "Don't worry. You'll get the hang of it."

"I'm not crying because my log books are messed up." Her laugh was watery. Her legs too weak to stand. She collapsed on the step of her truck and buried her face in her hands. *Get yourself under control, Jill.* This blubbering was so not like her. She was strong. God was her strength. But why did she feel so lonely? As though everything was suddenly falling apart?

The whole time King just stood there watching her blubber.

"I'm sorry. This isn't like me really. I'm just a little overwhelmed. And now I'm unloading this all on a stranger I've known for five days."

King glanced at his watch. "Six."

She hiccup laughed. "Six then." She twisted her fingers as the silence lengthened. Awkward.

CHAPTER FOURTEEN

King didn't know what to say. He started to reach out. Pat her arm or something. Anything besides watch her cry into her hands. His body refused to move, his hand halfway to the trembling shoulder. How could he, a man who had struck men in anger, and gone to jail for it, touch a woman as soft and beautiful as she? The tall lights touched the red in her hair, making a halo.

Once upon, even when talking came easier, he still didn't think he'd know what to say. He shifted through the pansy phrases that could comfort. But nothing fit. Especially after he had seen how well she had handled Marion's pain. What did he have to offer?

Midnight had come and gone and the dark was no place to rehash painful memories. Shadows grew deeper, regrets larger in the night. "Cadillac Ranch." *Where did that come from?*

She tipped her chin. "What?"

"You said you needed air. Cadillac Ranch is the place to get it, we can get some spray paint and stop on the way out of town tomorrow. Nothing but the smell of spray paint, cow manure, and desert dust for miles."

It was obvious his words puzzled her, but he didn't care, her teeth glimmered as a smile tugged at her lips. That's what he wanted. He loved her smile, it crinkled the corners of her chocolate eyes, rounding her cheeks. It lit her face and made a pretty visage downright beautiful. Wanting her to smile more he added. "Slapping a little graffiti around will get some stress out." He coughed, hiding a grin in his mustache. "Least that's what I've heard."

Finally, she laughed, the tinkling sound of ice

rain, without the dire consequences, of course. If he took the time to think about it, he might not be that far from the mark.

"What are you talking about?"

He feigned amazement and disbelief. "Don't tell me you've never heard of the Cadillac Ranch? I thought you were from Texas. I didn't think there was a Texan alive that didn't know about the eccentric art of Stanley March 3."

She stacked her hands on her hips and glared at him, unable to hide the twinkle in her eyes even in the dark. "First of all, I'm a transplanted Texan. You know the phrase, 'I got there as fast as I could'. But to tell the truth, I've never been more West than Dallas."

He shook his head. "Dallas. Pfft. Bunch a city folks forgettin' their roots. No. In the morning we'll stop by there and brand a few. That will perk you right up."

She laughed, this time it wasn't drowned in tears either. "Okay then. We'll do it." She took a deep breath. "Thanks again." Pausing, she added.

"Seems like I'm saying that a lot to you. You *are* a wonderful blessing to me."

He didn't want to spoil the mood by preaching at her against using her religion, so he reached down to pull her to her feet. He marveled at the rightness of the feel of her palm in his again. A sudden urge to protect her overwhelmed him. He stepped back and touched his hat to cover his confusion. "Anytime, Ma'am."

"Lead on, Loveless Leader."

He cocked his head. "Still trying out handles? I told you I don't need one."

Jill opened her door and flashed him a smile. "Nope. I just enjoy the name. It's different." Her face fell. "Not that I'm implying anything or mean —drat, if it offends you, I'll quit."

"Well, it sure beats King Snake." She blushed a dusky color in the dark. "But I save taking offense to bigger things."

"Like?"

He stepped over to his own truck. "Like not getting enough sleep." He hoped his smile took the sting out of the words. When she looked back, her smile mirrored his. For a long moment he admired her face, drawn in by the doe eyes almost hidden by glasses. He realized that he was staring like a sap and turned abruptly. He needed to watch himself. He could fall under this woman's spell and get lost forever. Then he'd really be on a hunt without a gun. *Not smart, King, not smart at all.*

***

She snuggled own into her sleeping bag, sighing. That man truly was one of the nicest she'd met. He didn't talk much, he protested he wasn't friendly, but if she made this trip alone, she would have fallen apart for sure. The tall cowboy was a rock, and she was certain he'd been put there by God.

And the way he looked at her, as though she were the prettiest woman in the world instead of a washed up ex-wife with grown kids, made her heart leap.

She reached for her Bible and this time found the courage to open it. The words she read by flashlight lifted her soul from the depths of despair. "Lord, forgive my arrogance and my fear." She prayed as her eyes began to droop. "Forgive my hardened heart. And thank-you for people like Shawn and King who make life just that much sweeter." She closed the Bible and her eyes. Visions of a hatted man followed her into her dreams. Such a tall drink of water in those starched jeans and crisp shirts. And those boots. She smiled as she drifted. She needed to ask him his secret. He never looked rumbled or stressed, whereas two days on the road left her feeling frizzy and drab. Plus he had the prettiest blue eyes that lit up when he talked. She loved the way he got animated about Cadillac Ranch. Whatever it was, she couldn't wait to see what the cowboy considered art.

Despite the hard floor and the coolness of the metal box truck, she slept better than she had in ten years.

CHAPTER FIFTEEN

Ten Cadillacs, multicolored tail ends sticking up like rooster tails, adorned the red dirt of the Texas plain. So this was art. The fickle April breeze promised a much hotter day than the one 12 hours earlier and 650 miles away, but it wasn't the weather creating the warmth that spread from her heart and showed in her smile.

"What color?" King proffered the spray paint cans like candy. His lips quirked into a mischievous smile.

She took one and shook it, trying to ignore the paint fumes from other intrepid artists competing with the cow pie aroma from the feedlot down the road. "Yellow. Nice and sunny."

King eyed the paint encrusted cars. "Good

choice." He chose red and placed the green and white on the ground by the truck. Then he popped the top and approached the nearest sedan like a man with a mission.

Jill hurried to catch up, admiring and envying the loose limbed walk that took the cowboy places at a good clip. "So now what?"

He stopped and turned. "Leave your mark."

She lifted her gaze higher, heat rising when she realized he'd caught her staring. She cleared her throat. "Anything?"

He shook the can hard, the mixer bead tapping back and forth. This guy meant business. "Sure. Anything."

King turned back to his car and stood poised, ready to spray. Nothing happened.

"Writer's block?"

He glanced over his shoulder. "No watching. Go on now, find your own spot."

She laughed at his growl, learning now that his bark was worse than his bite, and left him to his artistry. She ran her fingers along the heavily painted metal, tracing the lines of the writings from people who had come before. Some of the graffiti were hearts with initials, she liked the one that read 'we love our mothers'. Then there was the usual 'Sally was here', 'I love Jesus', and an ornate skull and cross bones with a pink bow and diamond eyes. Someone had spent a lot of time on that one.

She breathed deep of the warming air, looking back at the cowboy hat that bobbed with each arm movement. They should be moving, the delivery was still a day away, but King didn't seem in a rush today. Her heart thumped hard once as she thought about his kindness. The further he got from the yard, the more his angry, taciturn facade slipped away, revealing a warmhearted man of few words.

In the morning before leaving the truck stop, he'd helped with her log book. He drew on napkins the starts, weigh stations, fuel stops, and inspections, before she ever took pen to paper, saving her the time and aggravation of starting over or tearing out sheets. Which, of course, he lectured her on again when he saw evidence of several pages being ripped from the spine. The jagged edges torn in frustration were a dead giveaway.

And then *this* morning. A leisurely drive to the other side of Amarillo and this excursion to the famous public art exhibit of Stanley March 3. Over a quick coffee, King gave her his version of the history of the place. In 1974, an Amarillo billionaire got a hankering for an unusual type of art and had backed some art-hippies from California called The Ant Farm. As a tribute to the Cadillac tail fin, Cadillac Ranch was born. Not that any of the tail fins survived the vandals and trophy hunters, but the decorations added by passing sight seers had, and was even encouraged.

She blushed again thinking how she'd admired him walking to the cars. But it wasn't only that he was tall and good looking—for an older man that is. She smiled at herself. Not that she considered herself an older woman or anything. Nothing ever said gave her any of the bad feelings she should be getting if he was some kind of sociopath like Stu hinted. Quite the opposite in fact.

Just thinking of the other man and his many texts made her shudder. Thank goodness those had stopped when she changed her number. Of course, Shawn's usual good morning texts always came through. When she'd called him back, she couldn't stop herself from telling him about King when he got to worrying about her traveling with a strange man. It seemed to set his mind at ease. When she made her check-in call this morning to Marion, she'd informed him of how to get ahold of her, in case the company had to reach her. But now only Shawn, King, Marion, and her family had it.

Thinking of her son only added to the grin that began with the thoughts of the cowboy. The kid obviously wasn't angry at her, and she loved how he couldn't hold a grudge for more than a few hours. He may stew over words, but never over worthless feelings. Got in the way of analytical thinking he'd told her once. So, right on schedule, he told her good morning and to be safe.

Ducking out of the wind and barely avoiding a spinning dust devil, she set a tumble weed free and found a space painted mostly green on the the under chassis of a 1943 Club Sedan. She thought just a moment before painting Shawn with a sunshine around it. He was the light of her life.

But thoughts of her only boy led to thoughts of her daughter and cold claws chased away the warm fuzzies. The phone calls had seemed threatening to her. Shawn seemed to truly believe Stacy had changed. *Can I believe it?* Was she simply letting fear color her life? Her daughter was an adept liar, unabashedly bending truth or making up outright fiction to your face if it suited her ends—she always had. So could she be deceiving Shawn?

She sighed. Ten years was a long time. Look how much had happened in her life. A divorce, a new job. Now she caught herself ogling a man she'd only known a few days.

As though her thoughts conjured him, his voice sounded at the back of her head. "Want some brunch?"

She jumped up, whacking her head on the axle. "Ouch." She backed out from under the tilted car.

"That's going to leave a bump."

King backed away. "Sorry about that."

She shrugged. "I guess I was off in my own world." He didn't have to say it, but his look suggested maybe she did that a lot. She sighed. Maybe some explaining was in order.

"You have food with you?"

"I stocked my cooler. Plus I have a small camp stove. How does an omelet sound?"

She shook her head. "You're amazing. How do you carry all that stuff around?"

He tugged at his hat as though embarrassed to be called anything good. She'd have to remember to compliment him more. Every time she turned around he seemed to be doing something unexpected, but always kind.

"Okay. I guess the real question is, how will you get it back to the yard? Surely you can't take that on a plane."

He led the way through the gate, holding it open for a couple and their three kids, all armed with cans, before shutting it behind her. "Getting out of Phoenix is a little trickier than some other places. Renting a car works better than flying. Tickets are usually high outta there and getting to the airport is a pain."

"Oh." She'd only brought the barest items, not sure how she would get back to the yard. "Good thinking."

He disappeared into the brown box truck and reappeared with a suitcase that turned into a stove with a small side board. He set up everything near the back step of the UPS truck so he would have a platform. Next he retrieved his cooler and a back pack that stood nearly as tall as she. She'd seen those on soldiers in movies.

"Were you in the military?"

His hands froze over the cooler, then pulled out eggs, pre-chopped veggies, and a small carton of cream. In a mixing bowl he whisked it together and tossed it in the piping hot pan. It sizzled, filling the air with an aroma that even overpowered the chalky smell of dirt and hint of cow.

"No. Why?"

"The bag. It looks like something you see veterans packing as they go down the road or soldiers in movies." She studied him, hoping she wasn't trespassing. She'd hate for her over active curiosity to disturb the easy camaraderie developing between them.

"I was in Iraq for a time—contract driver." His deep voice rumbled lower, his mind far away.

"Oh. So you got it there?"

He flipped the omelet with a small spatula then dumped bottled water into a pot. That backpack must be bottomless to carry all those things. "No, army surplus. Kansas City. I did drive away before I got my rig."

"So that's how you know about getting around places."

"That. And the computer."

"You brought the computer too?"

He blinked at her. "Of course. Usually I use my phone for checking the board and finding flights, but the big screen is just better for some things. If I find a reload back, I need to print trip information."

"Don't tell me you have the printer too?"

He grinned. "No. I chose the stove instead. Here, grab those plates, it's almost done."

She went to the backpack and found a bag from the truck stop with a small package of paper plates, utensils, napkins, and foam cups.

She fished out two of each. "So where are the lawn chairs?" She teased.

For a moment he froze, as though he forgot something, then shook his head at her, motioning to the small space next to the stove. "Here you go, Madam, make yourself comfortable." He cut the omelet in half, slipped each onto the plates, then added coffee grounds to the hot water and poured her a cup without spilling a drop.

"That's heavenly. Thank you." She bowed her head for a moment of prayer, then breathed deep and took a bite. The eggs melted in her mouth, done to a turn with a hint of red pepper. "Wow, this is wonderful. You're a super cook. Even out here in the middle of nowhere."

King folded his long legs and hunkered to the

ground.

"Not only can you drive, massage out Charley horses, and conquer log books, you cook too." She watched him carefully, savoring another perfectly seasoned bite.

He ducked his head over his own food. "It's just eggs, Jill."

"Wonderful eggs. I don't know how you can't see it." she added gently, "but you really are a blessing."

He shrugged off her insistence. "Jus' eat."

She chuckled at him. "So what was it like over there?"

"Where?"

"Iraq." For a minute she thought she'd done it again, made him angry. His face closed off, fork pausing halfway to his mouth. He took the bite and raised his eyes to the horizon.

"It was everything they say it is, and worse."

CHAPTER SIXTEEN

King stared at the rainbow of Cadillacs, but the copper toned dirt of the Texas pasture turned to blood red sands of another country and he was whisked away to a time and place in his life he'd rather forget. Jill waited silent beside him and for the first time since being with the drivers over there, he wanted to talk about it.

"The gunfire was constant," he said finally.

Jill jumped as the words cut into the roar of the tractor trailers on I-40, and brought her back to reality. How long had he been lost in the memories? Abruptly drier than a year old bone, he took a drink. The luke warm liquid slid down his throat, easing the feel of a clogged esophagus. "The sand was everywhere. Your food. Your bed. Your shoes. You couldn't get away from it, no matter how you tried."

Jill froze, unwilling to break the spell, she could almost see his shell crack, giving her a glimpse of the man inside. His voice rumbled just below the sounds of the traffic on I-40 and she had to lean close to catch the soft words.

She reached out and touched his shoulder, trying to ease the palatable pain radiating like Texas heat waves.

He didn't heed the gesture. "The thing was—" He cleared his throat. "The thing was, I shouldn't have been there. I never should have left. I knew Carol wouldn't handle the separation. We'd been having troubles, but we needed the money, and it was good. My leaving got them killed." He turned back to her, his eyes blazing. "You see. I'm no blessing. I'm a curse. If I'd stayed home instead of chasing the dollars, Waylon and Carol would still be alive. She'd never have run off with the preacher to Africa and got killed in some civil war." He looked into his cup. "I've never told anyone that before."

So why he did now? It could be her soft presence. Her stillness that told him she listened with her soul, not just her ears. The warmth of the hand on his shoulder registered and he reached up to pat it awkwardly. When was the last time someone had touched him? The funeral? Nah, people had stared at him like wild calves. Then there's the whole house burning incident—but he wasn't about to unload that today. No, the patient woman beside him had to be done in with all his stories and reminiscing,

Jill stayed silent, heart aching for the man in front of her. She searched for words that would comfort him, but the words that came out surprised her just as much as they did him. "My daughter tried to kill me."

His gaze jerked to her. "What?"

"Some of my checks went missing. I thought I'd just misplaced them, then they started to hit the bank. Big checks at a beer barn and some electronics store. My account started bouncing, so I called the police and reported them stolen. Turned out my daughter's boyfriend had them. The police arrested him so she came after me." She touched the scar on her temple. "She beat me and set the house on fire—with me in it. I crawled out the back."

She shook herself to dispel the chill that crept into her soul. "I've never told anyone that either."

She chuckled. Here she sat on the back step of a UPS truck in the Texas wilds baring her soul to a stranger. But now they were even.

King shook his head at her. "How do you do it?"

"Do what?"

"Laugh. You're always laughing."

Heat rose to her cheeks. He honestly did think her a kook, laughing like a maniac at the littlest things. But the joy seemed to come easier around him, blessings more apparent. This big cowboy was so easy to talk to, and he listened with his whole body. She thought a moment, realizing her how important her answer was to this scarred man. "I know you don't want to hear it, but when things get as bad as they can, God always sends something my way to cheer me up. It took me forever to see it, but now I look for the funny in things, the blessings that tell me everything is in hands so much bigger than my own. Once I start laughing, well—life just gets better."

A car whipped by on the frontage road, the tailwind whipping off King's hat and sending it into the barbed wire fence. He leaped up and raced after it. He walked back, beating the dust off the already sad looking thing.

She grinned. "You have hair!"

The thick black locks lay plastered against his head, a contrast to the salt and pepper mustache. He plopped the hat back on as though embarrassed. "Of course I have hair. Just cuz I wear a hat doesn't mean I'm bald."

Jill dumped her empty plate into an old shopping bag. "Of course not. But you never take the thing off. I thought you might be hiding something."

"Well, I'm not," he groused. But his voice

lacked the snarly sound he used up North. He closed up the stove and repacked the backpack, while she cleaned up the food and put it away in the cooler.

When all was tucked back into the truck, King grabbed the last two cans of spray paint. "One more time before we hit the road?"

She grinned at him. Adding to the graffiti to the cars had a liberating effect. She eyed the five or six folks that had come while they were eating, some laughed and whooped, one young man hung halfway out of a car door in a macabre death scene while his friends took pictures.

She grabbed the white one. "Sure."

She headed back to her little spot under the sedan and next to her sunshine she wrote Stacy and then 'forgive'. Now it was perfect. Curious she headed over to King. He had found another spot a few cars down. He had written 'Remembered forever, Waylon'.

"Waylon? Your son?"

This time it was his turn to jump. "Yes, my boy." Tears pricked at her eyes and she swallowed them down. He must have loved his son so much. What kind of father had he been? Standoffish and growly? Or had he been different before? Those times when he was kind, she saw contrasting men than the one she had met in the training room. A man who had covered his hurt with a barrier the length and breath of the Great Wall of China.

She admired the way he handled the can easily. She held out her own stubby fingered hands for comparison. No matter how many teachers her mother had tried, these palms had never been able to span more than a few keys on any instrument. She'd barely been able to wrap around the spray paint.

With a flourish, he added a heart with the red and stood back. "Ready to get those monsters delivered?"

Obviously he didn't want to talk about it any more, so she nodded. "Just waiting for you."

He grunted. "Uh-huh."

She turned and trotted back to the trucks. "Last one there is the back door." She tossed over her shoulder. King had lead the whole way. It was her turn.

***

King watched her go and shook his head, a full grin creasing muscles unused before this trip. The woman was definitely trouble. Her view of God horribly skewed. How could she see blessings from Him, especially after everything she'd been through? He might have had people shooting at him, but that was war, no one he really knew. Her own daughter tried to burn her to death.

He climbed into the truck and pulled onto the frontage road and then the interstate. True to her word she made it to her truck first and took the lead. Just thinking of her challenge brought a quirk to his lips. Each time it came easier and easier, as if that deep numbness was on the thaw, as though the winter that had shriveled his heart and frozen his face in time and space, melted before her smiles and laughter.

She didn't even seem to blame God for the mess her life had become. That's what floored him.

She just took the blows, then got up and dusted herself off. He had to admit, her perky courage drew him. Even before he knew about her past, her attitude was catching, even to an old hater like himself.

He flipped the blinker down to pass a slow moving minivan with an overflowing baggage rack. Keeping a careful distance behind the other box truck so she knew he wasn't trying to steal her spot. Besides, the backdoor always seemed to get the better gas mileage.

He drummed his fingers on the steering wheel. Then there was this annoying habit she had of calling him a blessing, heaven sent, whatever. Why did she do that? Couldn't someone as good as she see the darkness on his heart. Should he tell her he'd been to jail? Not just for the short stint of burning his house down—that had been just a misunderstanding, but for drunkenness, brawling? Would she be so free with her smiles and laughter then? But even as he thought about telling her for the satisfaction it would bring, he envisioned the sorrow and mistrust in her eyes, her face falling, and he couldn't bring himself to finish out the scenario.

No, he didn't ever want to be the cause of crushing her hopes, but the silly woman needed to understand, he wasn't some knight in shining armor she seemed to think him—and she couldn't depend on him. When this run was over he needed to get as far away from her as possible, he didn't need or want her sunshine in his life.

The Texas sun warmed him through the windshield, his ribs softened thinking of the morning at Cadillac ranch and their impromptu picnic. Despite the sober turn of conversation, he'd enjoyed himself more than he had in forever. He would miss her some when they parted ways. The way her eyes crinkled and her smile widened when she saw her 'blessing' in something, her little snort that turned into unrestrained laughter—He needed to stop that train of thought immediately and get down to business. The problem with the driving business, however, is that it left the mind free to wander, and no matter how much he tried, he couldn't get it away from thoughts of Miss Mason.

CHAPTER SEVENTEEN

1200 miles and the last road block between her and her destination was a basketball shaped man waving his arms and a clipboard in the entrance. The man, satisfied that she wouldn't ram the gate—how could she with a barricade arm and ground spikes?—headed back into the shack off to the side. For a second she had the irrational thought of just flooring the little brown truck and forcing her way through. This was it, her first delivery, she just wanted to get it done and out of there.

With a pair of chain link gates topped by coiled razor wire the place looked more like a prison than than a hub of any sort. It gave her the shivers just looking at it, though beyond she could see a great deal of bustle. Rows of brown trucks and semis backed up to long rows of bay doors. Golf carts and people in the same drab color rushing between them.

She rolled down her window and peered at the guard shack.

Shadows scurried inside until the same basketball shaped man burst from the tiny door, shrugging into a jacket and waving a clipboard. "Stop, stop, you can't bring that in here." Okay, she was stopped. He didn't need to keep hollaring.

She slung open her door with the practice of over a thousand miles. He prevented her from pulling closer to the gates by positioning his body in the middle of the drive until he was sure he had her attention. She waved.

The little man's face turned from one of annoyance to dismay as he eyed the two idling trucks suspiciously. He approached hers first. "What are you doing? You can't bring those onto the grounds with gas in them."

Jill stared at him, not understanding. "We're here with deliveries from Indiana."

"You were due yesterday. That's when everyone else got here."

She tried to smile at him. "We got a late start. I had a flat tire."

"That's beside the point. You are not allowed on the premises with gas in them."

"Don't the trucks need gas to run?" Smart Alecky? Maybe—but the question had to be asked.

The man nodded. "Yes. But *you* aren't allowed to bring them on with over a quarter of a tank of gas. It's a fire hazard and a potential weapon."

Jill shook her head, not understanding. "A weapon?"

The man pointed his clip board at her and spoke as though she were slow witted. "Terrorists could use a truck to make a bomb and shut down this whole hub. Where would this area be without this service center?"

"Their mail would be late?"

He nodded. "It could shut down the whole system, mess things up for days. You have to get rid of your gas before you can bring those trucks in here." He glanced at his watch, "You'll need to get moving. Truck deliveries close at five."

"It's nine."

He glared at her. "And it takes a long time to inspect these things."

She got the feeling that the more she asked questions, the longer it would take to get the trucks through that gate. A glimpse of King's tall form in her rear view mirror sent a wave of relief spreading through her. He'd know what this was all about.

"What do you want us to do?" she asked.

The little man shrugged as he checked the truck numbers with a list on his clipboard. "The other drivers drove up and down the street until they were down to under a ¼ of a tank."

Jill stared at him. "They just drove around?"

"Yep."

King leaned a shoulder against the brown truck. "What seems to be the holdup?"

She pointed at the man. "He says we can't go in until we burn the gas down to a ¼ of a tank." Her disbelief must have showed in her voice because the basketball shaped man jutted his chin out belligerently and glared up at King.

"That's right. Security's orders and you drivers need to quit acting so shocked. Your company should have told you this."

King put up a hand. "Easy now, Friend, we don't want to start a ruckus. Generally drivers don't arrive with a whole lot of gas at the delivery because it's just a waste of our money, just give us a moment to figure out what we need to do."

The man blew out a breath on a sigh. "It's just everyone gets all upset when I tell you this. I don't have any control over the rules. I just have to make sure they're enforced." He stuck a hand out, as though remembering his manners. "You two are from Seas2Sea, aren't you?"

The cowboy gripped the basketball's hand. "Yes. Name's King. It's good to meet you."

"I thought I'd recognized those boots. I'm Phil.

So, she's in training now?"

The other driver shook his head. "No. She's got a handle on things."

Jill straightened in her seat. The last few hundred sweaty miles had been well worth it.

The other man wasn't so impressed with King's praise. "Well, you need to have people explaining things better in training, she tried to barge right through the gate. We do have security measures I have to maintain."

Jill simmered at the unfairness of his accusations. He acted like she planned to mow everything down. A twinge of guilt pricked her. The thought *had* gone through her head.

He tapped his board then pointed at her with his pen. "When you have the correct amount of fuel, you may drive to dock two." He motioned to King. "And you're at six. Exit your vehicle and go to your left. You will see signs and arrows to the driver's waiting area. Go directly there and do not leave until you have been released to do so. There was a threat last year, you know."

Jill swallowed. Maybe she should take him a little more seriously. "Here?" Her voice squeaked a little. "What kind of threat? Why here?"

The little man puffed up like a kitten and his voice turned scathing. "No, not here. The threat was in New York, an arsenic like substance was found at the bottom of a brand new truck. The whole hub had to be evacuated."

Jill frowned. "But I thought you said that happened in New York."

The man gritted his teeth until she cringed at the sound. "Yeah. So. It could happen here so we have rules for drivers."

Jill nodded, just hoping to pacify the guy. He seemed antsy.

He nodded and pointed, repeating his instructions while King walked back to his truck.

"Of course you don't, we don't want to get you in trouble," said Jill.

The man's face changed to one of relief. "Thanks guys. Our security team has been all over this hub. Making inspection, sometimes three times a week to check the trucks."

A large door in the building behind them started opening and the back up alarm of another brown truck warned of one backing out.

The man turned at the sound. "No, no, no," he yelled, jogging off, "I said bay three, not two."

Jill smiled as she watched him go. "He has a rotten job."

King nodded.

"Okay, so what do we do?"

"Since all my siphoning stuff is in my truck, I guess we're driving until the gas light comes on. Whatcha got?"

Jill tapped her dash. "Just under a half."

"It's an hour or two of driving then, we'd better get to it."

It took two hours of circling. Stopping and starting as various trucks of all sizes came and went. After the first hour she began to wonder if it was a conspiracy. Two smaller trucks came in from a different company and joined the brown carousel, the four trucks following nose to tail. Jill yawned.

Add tinkling music and they could work a fair.

King pulled along side of her and honked once when he hit his mark, but she still had a some to go, so he went ahead and checked in while she circled. Another truck went in, then the other. Jill thumped her dash. The light dinged on and the needle dropped a couple of ticks. *Made it.*

***

Jill eased the truck into the indicated bay and followed the directions to the letter. The driver's lounge was a small box of a room with a plastic round table, a few chairs, a vending machine, and a large sign that read 'Drop Paper Work Here' just above a slot in the wall. She secured the envelope with a quick lick and dropped it in. She sighed and stepped aside so King could do the same. A weight seemed to lift from her shoulders. She had done it. Her first load was in the bay. She threw herself back into the blue vinyl seat, uncaring of the slight smell of emu oil from someone's hair care product with the lemon smell of cleaner over the top. *Thank you, Lord.*

Once again she was exhausted from head to toe. Who would have known that this job, one that she spent most of her time sitting, would be so tiring.

"I did it. Got my first load delivered."

King chuckled as he settled in the chair beside her. "Oh, we're only about half done."

Jill straightened. "What do you mean?"

"Check-ins can, and usually do, last several hours."

She sighed and leaned back. "I feel like I've been run over by my own truck a few times."

King laughed again. She liked that sound.

He flipped out his phone and started tapping at it. "It'll get easier. Check-in is a good time to figure out how to get back to the yard."

"Oh no. I totally forgot." With everything going on, it never crossed her mind. "So what are you doing?"

"I'm renting a car." He looked up finally and seemed to take pity on her. "Cuts costs to share if you want."

The heat climbed to her face. She should have thought this through. Should she try to go on her own? She didn't have to ask herself twice. "I'd love that."

He nodded and went back to his phone. "Okay."

She wanted to say more, how much she enjoyed the trip down, despite all the drama with her daughter. . .and the panic attacks. . .and—

Her phone rang before she could continue beating herself over the head and make the situation even more awkward than it was.

"Hello."

"Hi Jill." *Stu.* "There seemed to be something wrong with your phone for the longest time. I had to check with the people at the office on the number and Elaine, you remember Elaine, right? She told me you'd changed it."

"I had to change it for safety reasons. No one should have given it out." She definitely needed to have to have a word with this woman when she got back. Stu continued as though he hadn't heard her.

"Are you on your way back yet?"

"Not yet. Just waiting on the inspection."

"Then what?"

"Well. I guess it's another load and on the road again."

King stood and moseyed over to a cork board beside the vending machine as though to give her privacy. Her eyes followed him. He always seemed to think of her, it made her like him even more. She tried to focus on Stu's words. Why was it so hard? She wouldn't mind never hearing from the other driver again for that matter. Talking to King was so much more relaxing than Stu's pushing and prodding.

But Stu didn't miss a beat and continued with his mostly one-sided conversation. "I'm just heading in myself. If you rent a car you could be back in a couple of days. I'll wait for you and then we can take a load together, sound okay?"

Jill was silent for a moment, debating if she wanted to run with him. But she had liked making this trip with King, his knowledge and his comfort with getting in and out of places had helped speed things along. She also felt safe traveling with him. A run with someone else who knew the ropes could only help, right?

"Jill?"

"Sure, that sounds good, it'll take me some time to get up there, so if you find a load you need to take, go ahead." She couldn't shake the uneasiness she felt when she thought of Stu, his messy truck compared to Kings' and his insistence they should run together.

"Oh, don't worry, I'll wait for you. King still with you?"

Jill glanced at her partner as he settled into a seat and pulled his cowboy hat low for a nap. "Yes."

His voice lowered to a whisper. "Just be careful, Jill."

His warning rankled at her. *Did he even know King besides by reputation?* "Okay, bye." She hung up and tried to get comfortable, but the seat seemed to be too big in every way. Finally she brought her feet up and stuffed her sweater behind her back. *Ah, that's better.* She reached for her Bible. She'd gotten behind on her daily devotions with this crazy schedule. She had promised herself that wasn't going to happen. She'd found that when she stopped reading the Bible, bad things followed in quick succession.

King settled back into his chair and tipped his hat over his eyes. His voice seemed strange, almost jealous. "Stu again?"

She answered automatically though her mind was on the way he spoke. "Yes."

"How'd he get your new number?"

Jill frowned. "He said a lady gave it to him. Elaine?"

King shrugged. "Don't know her. Seems odd, his calling all the time."

His position seemed to muffled the words, but she caught a catch in his voice. As though he had a lot more to say about her relationship with Stu but bit his tongue instead. Still, she felt compelled to defend the other man, though it rubbed her wrong for him to have her new number. And that it was just handed out as though he were a close friend or next of kin.

"He's just making sure I'm okay. My dispatcher, Marion, and Sam have each called too."

"But not as often as Stu?"

"No. He wants to coordinate a run together, that takes checking in a few times."

King grunted. She thought about saying more, but the cowboy seemed to drift off. She simmered a moment, then chuckled at herself for reading too much into a few simple words and reached for her Bible. Taking a nap sounded good, but she had resolved to read through the Bible this year. That was before she realized being on the road could be so exhausting. She'd figured she'd have lots of time to relax and read. Boy had she been wrong.

She checked the schedule she'd pulled off the internet and kept folded in the back flap of the cover. She'd missed two days this week plus today and needed to read Job 39-40, Psalms 57-59, II Samuel 15-19, and Exodus 25-28. She got a highlighter out and got to work. Marking off each day as she read, another piece of paper allowed her to jot down her thoughts if something special struck her.

"Be merciful unto me, O God, be merciful unto me: for my soul trusteth in thee: yea, in the shadow of thy wings will I make my refuge, until these calamities be overpast." She read as she moved into Psalms. Just what she needed after Stacy's calls and a sleepless night.

Somehow this schedule seemed to always have the right words to soothe her soul. She knew it was all in God's plan, but it was good to be reminded of it when her mind churned so crazily. Her thoughts kept coming back to King. She liked this crusty cowboy. A lot. But even if he cared for her in return, what was the future?

The sleepless night begin to catch up with her, along with the relief the words provided. She rested her Bible on her knee while she closed her eyes for a moment.

CHAPTER EIGHTEEN

King watched the peacefulness steal over Jill's face as she read her Bible. The tenseness and exhaustion that had been on it all day, faded, and she slept. The Bible tipped open. He craned his neck to see what had brought such relief. Her pen pointed to a verse.

"My soul is among lions: and I lie even among them that are set on fire, even the sons of men, whose teeth are spears and arrows, and their tongue a sharp sword." That sure described people, especially Christians, perfectly. His lips curled into a wry smile as he thought of the women in his old congregation. "Teeth like spears" fit them to a 'T'.

"Would you like to borrow it?" Jill asked, eyes still closed.

"Nah, just curious is all about what made you go to sleep so fast. I can see now."

Jill's eyes snapped open then narrowed. "The Bible didn't put me to sleep, a sleepless night on that shelf did. These words are a balm to my soul."

"Help with the panic attacks?"

She turned pale at his words and he realized how mean they sounded. Why did he let things like that pop out of his mouth? "I just meant that you seem to have them and if it helps that's good. I don't want you driving off the road or anything."

She relaxed, but her words were ground out between clenched teeth. As though she said them a lot, probably to herself. "I don't have panic attacks. I'm past that."

"Okay." King shrugged he'd let her believe that if it helped.

"Why do you wear that hat anyway?"

That made him laugh. "You're trying to change the subject. I've been to Iraq remember? I've seen all forms of PTSD—even went through a spell myself. Besides, it was the only thing I saved from the fire when my house burnt."

Great, now she felt bad about making fun of his hat. "I'm sorry."

He shrugged. "Don't be, it was my own darn fault. I got to burning old photos, well everything of my ex-wife's really, and fires in the middle of a Texas drought don't go well together."

Jill laughed, despite herself. He delivered his speech in such a deadpan voice she could just imagine the angry cowboy doing some sort of ancient war dance around a fire as it burned out of control. The laughter hurt her tightly wound insides.

She sighed. "My daughter's calls tend to upset me, that's all. She's written me a letter, telling me she was getting out and wanted to know where I was, and for some reason Shawn, my son, gave her my phone number. Originally she was only sentenced to 3 years because she plea bargained to testify against Smokey. But something happened in prison, I really don't know what. Some problem with her attitude or something and she got more time. Now she's out, I'm afraid she wants to find me."

"So you ran."

"What?"

He nodded to himself. "That's why you took this job isn't it? Traveling all over the country."

Jill froze. *This is what happens when you spill your guts to people, you ninny.* They figure out what a fake you are and what's really going on. How you're too afraid to let God take care of it, how you're so afraid of your daughter you will do anything, including dropping everything, and running. Anger at herself boiled in her gut, bitter acid that ate up her esophagus and sent her heart into rapid fire mode.

She jumped up to start pacing, to get away from the thoughts that shortened her breath. Blindly she looked for the door, but she didn't get far.

A warm hand curled around hers and then an arm around her shoulder. "Hey, hey. Don't get upset. I'm sorry. I don't know why my mouth shoots off like that. Just thinking out loud."

She knew that. So why did she have to go all panicky on him. Still, his hug felt good. Too good. She melted into his arms, burying her face into the soft cowboy shirt, trying to forget what had brought her here. The tension eased from her shoulders. She took a steadying breath before looking up into the concerned face of her partner.

"I'm sorry." She seemed to be saying that a lot lately. How could she ever get control of her life again if simple conversations set her off into a panic? There was only one answer she knew. Help me, Lord.

King brushed a hair away from her glasses. "Better now?"

She nodded. He always knew what to do, what she needed. He must have a lot of experience with panic attacks. Did he hug everyone? She hoped not. She felt special wrapped in his arms.

The door opened and a cough made her aware that she was in the tall man's arms. She jerked back. He let her go. Immediately, she missed the strength and warmth of his hug. She looked at the guard who had originally barred her entrance.

He fidgeted at the door. "Your trucks are finished. Go across the hall to the office and Tina will have your paper work."

"Thank-you," she managed.

He nodded and disappeared. She turned back to her bags on the floor, avoiding the cowboy's eyes, but his hand touched her shoulder.

"Jill, you should talk about this. It helps."

"To you?" She demanded.

He seemed surprised by the question and his hand slipped from her shoulder. "It doesn't have to be me. Someone who knows about PSTD—"

"Been there. Done that. I'm all better." She swiped at her eyes.

He stepped away and reached for his own well packed duffle.

He glanced down when his phone whistled. "Car's ready. I'd say that was perfect timing." When he looked at her there was no condemnation in his eyes. Nothing that told her he thought she'd lost her marbles. Had she imagined his jealously? The way he had pulled her into his arms?

She focused on gathering her own scattered belongings to hide her confusion. One minute he was all kindness, the other distant. Then again, it didn't help her falling into his arms after knowing him all of a week. What kind of thoughts must be going though his mind about the kind of person she was? Why she'd let it happen anyway? King was her partner for this trip. He'd made it plenty clear that he didn't often do this so the probability of her actually running with him or even seeing him again was pretty slim. She needed to pull herself together. Get past these fears about Stacy finding her, and leave the poor man alone.

She shifted her bag on her shoulder. Suddenly weary and a little saddened at not seeing King again. Still, that was at least three days away. In the meantime, she needed to figure out what to do about Stacy. From her past therapy sessions she knew a decision on the matter would go a long way to settling her fears. Shawn said she wanted to talk.

Maybe she should. Maybe she needed to give her daughter the chance that she had changed instead of running scared like she was.

Jill took a deep breath of the spring air as the cab dropped her and King off at the agency. Still, this freedom of moving across the country couldn't be beat. In the last week she done more traveling than she had in 15 years. To top it off she was getting paid for it. No matter what happened, she knew she'd keep this job.

She admired the tall cowboy as he walked out flipping the keys to a car. He pointed to a blue Jetta and she gathered up her things one more time. They had already agreed to split the cost of car and fuel going back. Would he want to drive the whole time?

He slipped into the driver's seat while she tossed her things in the back and she tried to hide her smile. Men. Some things never changed.

CHAPTER NINETEEN

Like a copperhead in the dry summer leaves, the smoke crept into the car through the vents. So insidious at first that King didn't even notice it. Ahead, the sky hazed over, the chill of the fickle spring weather belied by the heat waves on the road. Tractor trailers slowed, brake lights flashed dull in the thickening haze and warning signs flapped in the ever present wind. He snapped closed the vents, but it wasn't fast enough or thorough enough. The car reeked of hot summer wind and grass fire though the temperatures were cool.

Beside him, Jill stirred but did not awake. She'd

fallen asleep just before they turned East onto I-40 and had lain quiet ever since. But now she moaned in her sleep, a low distressed sound, the weak call of a blind kitten. Her brows scrunched towards her nose, lips drawn down in one of the first frowns he'd ever seen on her face. Even when she talked about her daughter she hadn't looked like that. He turned his attention back to the road. Emergency vehicles lined the sides, waving the sluggish traffic through the smoke. Bright fires burned in the distance, but they were small, controlled.

King relaxed back in his seat. Just a controlled burn before wildfire season hit. He'd watched the news last summer while the West burned out of control, whole communities losing everything, some never to revive. Jill shifted again, obviously upset by something. Should he reach over and wake her? The smoke got thicker, the markers on the road guiding beacons for the slow traffic.

"Come on, people, Keep it moving." Rubberneckers. Always snarling simple situations and making jams worse. He took a deep breath and tried to get comfortable in the tiny car. His knees thumped on the steering wheel again.

The smoke in the small space began to clear, pure unfiltered daylight ahead, but the lady next to him acted distressed, as though caught in a dream she could not escape. The tiny sounds ripped at his soul.

Unable to watch her suffer with her dream any longer, he touched her arm. "Jill?"

She screamed and bolted upright, eyes wide, had batting the smoke from her face. "No!"

The smoke cleared completely, King cracked his window and then the back on opposite side. A fresh breeze shifted through the car, chasing the haze away. He kept his eyes on the road, but watched her carefully. She seemed awake now.

"You okay?"

Wide eyes blinked uncomprehending from behind glasses sitting skew on her nose. "Where are we? I smelled smoke?"

He jerked a thumbed over his shoulder. "Rangers burning off the winter tinder."

She took a deep breath and sank back down, shifting as though the seat had turned into a mound of fire ants then finally settled back, wiping at a tears that leaked from the corner of her eye. If he didn't know any better, definitely a severe case of PSTD. He'd seen plenty of that, even suffered from it himself, he was told. That daughter of hers must had done a number on her. Was she even safe to be out on her own like this? What would happen when he wasn't around to wake her out of her dreams? He chuckled to himself. Who did he think he was? She'd most likely do what everyone else did— scream herself awake and then deal with it.

"You with me now?"

She put a shaking hand to her brow and took a steadying breath. "Yes. I'm sorry about that." She twisted to look back. The wall of smoke looked like a fog bank now as traffic picked up and moved on towards Amarillo at a more reasonable speed. She chuckled as though embarrassed. "I hope I didn't scare you."

His mouth lifted in a half smile. "It'd take a

little more than that, Ma'am."

She offered him a shaky smile. "Well, yes. I guess it would."

For a moment silence fell, he knew he shouldn't, but he asked anyway. "Dream about your daughter?" Boy wasn't he just Chatty Cathy?

She turned to him, brows raised in a silent question. He resisted the urge to hunch his shoulders and hide against his door. She made it so easy to ask questions? To talk. Since he'd unloaded his Iraq story and she'd let him in on her ugly past, it seemed as though a two way line of communication stayed open all the time. Her quiet acceptance seemed to have freed his tongue.

Then there was the hug in the driver's room at the UPS hub. What had possessed him to do that? But she hadn't seemed to mind. Hadn't pushed him away like he deserved. She was too good, too soft, too everything good that a man who caused the death of his wife by ignoring her and taking off to Iraq deserved. But she had felt so right in his arms. Despite her small stature, they had fit so well.

Jill stared out the window. "I don't think so. I don't remember the dream. I was in the house, surrounded by smoke, and knew I had to get out of there. But I couldn't," she shrugged as though it wasn't a big deal, "so I burned."

That would explain the scream.

"Don't worry though. The therapist I visited for a while after the incident fixed me up. She said I needed to try some lucid dreaming and dream myself getting out of the house."

"But you did--make it out before you burned right?" He didn't see any scars.

She touched a thin line on her temple. "I did. I don't know how." Her voice whispered, taunt with painful memories. "I remember crawling across the carpet. The kitchen was torture. It was linoleum, you know, nothing to grab onto. I had to stand and let the counter hold me up. I prayed and the next thing I knew I'm falling out the back door. My neighbor helped me from there."

She stared out the passenger window. "Later the doctor said I had two broken ribs, one cracked clavicle, a broken arm and a finger where she stomped on it." She took a shaking breath and faced him square, as though she knew he wouldn't want to hear what she'd say next. "I don't remember crossing the ten feet to the backdoor. I know in my heart that an angel carried me. That God answered my prayer."

Her tiny chin jutted at him, as though daring him to dispute her words with his bitter vitriol, just itching for a fight. He didn't give it to her. He envisioned her bloody, broken body lying on the floor, her last coherent breath a prayer to her God to save her.

He nodded slowly. "Then He did."

King made sure his eyes stayed fastened on the blacktop ahead, but a side ways glance revealed a quiver in the determined chin and the fight deflate right out of her. Who in their right mind would object to someone thinking an angel saved them? She was sitting next to him wasn't she? The argument in his head went on until he realized what he was doing. Trying to justify God stepping in to save Jill when there had been no one to save Carol and Waylon.

The pain stabbed at his heart again. Reminding him that if there was a Man upstairs, he certainly didn't take any interest in King or his life. He glanced at the little woman beside him as she shifted deeper in her seat and tried to get comfortable. He could see why God would save her though. She held onto His hand through it all.

"I just wonder why He didn't save Carol or Waylon," he said into the silence. "I know why he saved you. You're a good woman, Jill. But God spared me in Iraq where people took pot shots at me, and I should've died. And then Carol goes off with a pastor and winds up dead." He stared straight ahead, unwilling to look at the person beside him, the one he had just bared his soul to, until a soft hand touched his leg.

***

Jill stared at the iron jawed man. Could she get any more insensitive? Why was she talking about God saving her, when his wife and child had died terribly in a far off land? The only thing that gave her a clue to the depth of his emotion were the white knuckles on the steering wheel.

"I'm sorry, King. Nobody knows—"

"I know what you're going to say. That nobody knows the hour. There's a season for everything." He glanced at her, storm-cloud eyes bleak. "Believe me, I have heard them all. Friends, not quite friends, even enemies all say the same thing over and over. But it makes no sense. None of it. Why'd your daughter try to kill you? You didn't deserve that. Why did Waylon have to die? What kind of God would let that happen?"

Jill shook her head, wanting to help this hurting man so badly. " Not God, King. Put the blame were blame is due, the devil and our own terrible life choices. I married violent men, but all the warning signs were there. I brought children into homes that were hateful and abusive. I can't begin to imagine your pain, but mine is from my own choices." Her voice dropped to a whisper as she talked more to herself than to him as the guilt from all her failures pressed down on her. "But I do know that God forgives us and wants to make things better. I just have to claim the promises and I try to do that every day. Take it one day at a time." As soon as the words left her mouth and she claimed the truth of forgiveness a peace settled over her and she was able to relax back into her seat. Her shoulders eased and she smiled. Only a loving God could give her this feeling and she prayed King would find it himself soon. Then he truly would be the perfect man. She frowned. Maybe that wouldn't be so good, she already liked him enough as it was.

CHAPTER TWENTY

The tension in the car slowly dissipated and his hand dropped from the wheel to cover hers. "Here I'm counseling you to talk to someone and I end up unloading my baggage on you."

She left her hand in his. "I guess we're both guilty of unloading on each other this trip. I sure hope I have it out of my system. But you are right, about talking about it. I always feel better after we do. I did talk to my therapist. But that was years ago. After that—" She glanced up at him through her lashes, "I didn't want to unload my baggage on unsuspecting friends."

He nodded. "I guess I deserved that. Like I said afore—I run off with my mouth sometimes."

"And here I thought you were the stand offish type. King Snake and all."

Now he laughed outright. *How did she do that?* She sure knew how to get under a man's skin. A sign caught his eye, the only green in the brown landscape.

"Albuquerque's up ahead."

She straightened. "How long have I been sleeping?"

He chuckled. "A few hours. You stirred when I stopped, but never spoke up so I just kept going."

Rubbing her face she stretched in the seat. "Wow. I didn't realize how tiring this job could be."

"Don't worry, you do get used to it." He refrained from mentioning the severe emotional stress accompanying her this trip. Looking for an excuse to escape the confines of the car and get a breather from the protectiveness she inspired in him, he pulled off the interstate for fuel. Not that the efficient vehicle needed another stop, but he sure did.

"Where are we?" asked his companion as she eyed the dusty landscape.

"Grants is straight ahead a few miles, but this is a good place to stop a while. There's not so much of those diesel fumes that seem to go to your head."

Jill ducked her chin at his reference to her late night walks to get away from things, but she smiled all the same. She peered up to the sign near the wide of the road, ragged from a recent storm. "Sign looks like I feel. Some sort of outpost, but the letters are all gone." She flashed a smiled at him. "Ah well, I'll trust you this isn't some cheesy tourist trap."

"Now I didn't say anything about that—Just a good place to stop."

"It looks interesting. It's my turn to pay for the gas so I'll go in and get it started. Need anything?"

"Naw. I'm alright."

"Okay. I'll be back in a minute."

After a moment, the station beeped and he topped off the tank. Jill had not reappeared, so he moseyed inside to wait. For a few minutes, he wandered aimlessly among the imported trinkets from Mexico and shelves of fireworks, moving towards the back and off to the side noticed a gift store tucked towards the back he'd never noticed during previous visits.

He jerked his head towards the door. "You add something new?"

The clerk shrugged. "Awhile back. Some local stuff from the reservation."

Still no sign of Jill, so King stepped through glass entry with a vinyl cut out of a dream catcher. Most of the stuff was the usual high priced trinkets, rainbow serapes, dream catchers from key chain size to take up the whole wall monstrosities—How would those even fit in a normal sized car? There were plastic bows and arrows, sculptures with scantily clad women and horses, and a lot of wolves. Tchotchkes with nothing Native American about them.

A lighted jewelry counter and the glint of a beaten silver necklace in the display cabinet caught his eye. It was a simple thing, rectangular with a primitive sun punched into pendant.

He motioned to the attendant, half hidden in a corner with a cash register, "Could I see that?"

The young lady looked up from her phone with a sigh. "It's open, just slide it."

King reached over and did just that, thankful for his long arms. The necklace swayed gently on a delicate strand of woven twine, the beaten silver glinting as it caught the overhead light. The back of the rectangle had been overlaid with gold so the raised glinted with a hint of sun fire. The gray metal almost obscured the gilt, but instead brought it out, almost giving it a golden hue, like the sun peeking out from behind a cloud. Once in his large palm the piece was heavier than its delicate appearance suggested. So *her*.

His fascination with the trinket seemed to catch the attendant's attention. She put her phone down and approached hesitantly.

"Do you like it?"

"I do."

She beamed, laying a ring encrusted hand on the

glass. "I made it. The manager lets me put a few pieces out since I'm working on my jewelry design degree online." The rings on her fingers each had a wholesome, simplistic look like the medallion in his hand. She looked down, seeming to realize her words tumbled out of her. "I don't sell many though."

Just a few days ago he wouldn't have cared about this vulnerable young lady's self esteem struggle, in fact he never would have stepped into the little store connected to the travel center. How many times had he stopped here, fueled and moved on, his only goal to keep on the road and keep the pain at bay? He stared at the top on the bent head, brassy red dye dull in the harsh light.

"I'll take it. I think you have talent." The words fell stilted from a tongue long unused to compliments, and the way she looked up reminded him so much of Waylon after a simple praise, he nearly choked and left the necklace on the counter.

"You do?"

He nodded. "Sure. And handmade just makes it

all the more special, doesn't it?" He just couldn't stop after he started.

She nodded and took the chain. "I think so. We don't got no boxes to put it in, but I can see if there's a cigarette box out back."

"Naw. That's okay." Obviously she wanted to do something special, but both of them were at a loss.

Finally she wrapped it in some paper towels and put it in a tiny bag. "Thank-you. You're my first sale."

He touched his hat. "Honored, Ma'am."

Her eyes shot down to the cash register, but not before he caught the little smile of pride on her face.

He'd just handed over the cash when Jill stepped through the door as though she'd been looking for him.

"There you are." She looked around the little shop, and then back at him. She'd never caught him browsing before and it was obvious she was curious as to what would bring him into this particular place. "What a cute shop. It smells like pine."

Guiltily, he stuffed the cash back in his pocket and hid the bag in his shirt pocket. The clerk looked from him to Jill with a knowing smile, but she didn't say anything.

"It's nice enough for a tourist trap." He said in a rush of breath. "Ready to hit the road again?"

"I think I can handle a few more hours if you can."

That's his girl, always ready to rise to a challenge. He cringed. Where did he get that? Calling her his girl? He was just glad he hadn't said it out loud. Along with complimenting complete strangers, things like that were to close to skipping off his tongue and creating even more awkward situations. However, he did like the way the last awkward situation had ended. In fact, Jill had a way of making difficult discussions end well in the long run.

His blood nearly boiled over when he thought of the girl that had beat her to the ground and tried to kill her. Nearly put out the sunshine before it could even enter his life. His heart clenched as he thought of her leaving him in just two more days. Taking the sunshine and light out of his life.

As he got into car, the bag crinkled like a snake in the grass every time he moved, reminding him it was there and that it was just as dangerous as a rattler. Every so once in a while, he touched it, not sure how to brooch the subject or how to give it to her. Why had he even bought the thing? Now he had this hot spot over his heart. Just like the little woman by his side, thawing that protective shell he'd built. What an idiot.

He ignored her sideways look though he could tell she'd seen him touch the package, and that the curiosity was killing her.

Finally she asked. "Did you find anything good in the little shop? I didn't get a good look around, but it seemed like a nice place. You seemed in a real hurry to get going again." He stifled a smile. So it was his fault she hadn't gotten to look around. Didn't the woman realize that if she wanted to take a day in that little shop he would have waited? No, best not to let her know she had that sort of power over him.

He nodded, grabbing at the opening like a bronc rider at a pickup man. "It had a few nice things. I found something that kind of fit you."

She squirmed and when he managed another look her way, her eyes glowed behind her glasses. "You did?"

"Sure. You said you were looking for a handle —" He handed her the crackly package, wishing at the last minute he had been able to find a box and wrapped it. Something glittery done up with delicate bows The lady deserved so much more that a paper towel wrapped trinket in some generic thank-you bag.

She took it as reverently as though he'd handed her a box of fine chocolates. "Oh." Her gaze turned suspicious. "You said Hot Shots didn't have handles."

Stupid man, always running your mouth. "Some people just earn them."

She paused in opening the packet and eyed him with a frown. "Wait a minute. I didn't earn something like 'Lost Lackey' or 'Shortleg' did I?"

He chuckled. "Open it and find out."

She began and then paused again. "Then again, Leadfoot might get me more loads if the dispatchers know I'll get it there on time."

She was killing him. "And more tickets."

Once again she stopped and started. This time he caught her wicked sideways look in her and realized she baited him. "You could have warned me I was earning a handle. Should there be some sort of ceremony? Like dumping Gatorade over me or something? Not that I think that would be any fun, but—"

"That's football." He throttled the steering wheel as doubts plagued him. What if she didn't like it? It wasn't anything fancy. Perhaps more thought on this spur of the moment gift was in order. Like she said, women liked ceremony. *Too late for that.*

While he agonized over her slowness, she opened the towels. Her breath hitched. "A sun. It's gorgeous." She stared at it a moment. "But what is the handle to go with it?"

His button collar tried to strangle him all of a sudden and he coughed. He might think it easily enough, but saying it to her turned out to be something else all together. "Sunshine," he finally sputtered, mangling the word with a croak.

Her smile, soft with anticipation before, broke loose, growing until her eyes crinkled behind her glasses, lashes glittery with tears. Oh darn, now he'd gone and made her cry. He couldn't seem to get anything right.

Once upon a time he'd thought himself pretty smooth with the ladies. Obviously, it wasn't a skill that stuck if unused. He couldn't talk with any sort of sense or do anything right.

"My handle is Sunshine?"

He nodded, not trusting himself to speak again.

She didn't speak for a long time either, looking at the trinket and holding it up to catch the last red hued light of the spring sun. It dipped below the flat horizon, one last ray gleaming off the side mirror and touching the gold back of the pendent. Her face was turned away. He had no clue of the thoughts going through her mind.

"You don't have to keep it or anything." He assured her. " I just—"

"It's perfect. Really. I just don't know how you can think such a nice thing after all my drama this last week. I'm not usually like that, but unfortunately that's all you've gotten from me. Not a very good way to earn such a sweet name."

"That drama isn't you. The sun fits you ."

"Thank-you." She rolled the word around. "Sunshine. I like it. I'll try to live up to it."

"Bosh. There's no living up to it. Like I said, you are it. You—" He grasped for those suave words that always seemed to elude him. Being mean came easily, but he had to tell her how he felt. So many people had beaten at her self-esteem, she had no clue as to how wonderful she was. "When you enter a place, you bring the sunshine with you." No way could he tell her how many years he'd been so cold, frozen in place behind his wall of manly gruffness, how her presence ripped through his life like a solar storm. How could he name something even he didn't understand.

***

Jill stared at the cowboy beside her, completely undone by his sweet words. There was no way this man was the type that Stu warned her about. So then the question remained, what kind of game was the other man playing? Unwilling to ruin this moment with that type of thought, she reached for one of the hands hanging onto the steering wheel with a death grip. To her surprise, he gave it to her.

"Thank-you so much. This is truly one of the most meaningful gifts I have ever been given." He shifted, seemingly uncomfortable with the amount of emotion in the car again so she released his hand. She gave him what she hoped was a teasing smile. "No matter what anyone else says about you, I still think you're a blessing."

He opened his mouth for his usual vitriol, but she held up her hand.

"Nope. Not going to hear it and there's no way you can deny it any more. But don't worry. Your secret's safe with me."

He stared ahead at the road, but her heart swelled to see the soft little smile playing under his mustache.

CHAPTER TWENTY ONE

Jill popped out of the car at the Cuba Missouri Flying J. Boy, that had been a long stretch. Sometimes King drove like a machine, straight through and without a word. She didn't castigate him too hard, though, the pendant warmed the hollow of her throat. The gesture of giving her a handle said more than any amount of chit chat could. Not that King spent a whole lot of time on worthless words. The touch of a hand, taking her to Cadillac ranch, these all said so much more that those types of things ever could.

The thoughtful gift and his compliments even

now made the heat climb to her cheeks.

Her light thoughts added a skip to her steps and she fairly bounced up the curb. She stopped in her tracks when the form of a body lying in the shadows caught her eye. A large man lay draped across a bench between the ice box and a side door, mostly hidden by the double door freezer. Black clothes, black shirt over a black vest with the bare glimmer of colored patches. A bandana covered the top of his head and whiskers formed a mask which completed the camouflage, so much so that she wouldn't even have noticed him if he hadn't shifted in his sleep as she approached. What looked to be a cardboard sign rested on the gentle swell of his chest, rising and falling under his clasped hands.

Hovering between the light of the station, the promise of warm food and shelter so close for those with the cash, she bit her lip. But what about those without? What about those who lurked in the shadows, hungry? She didn't know what his sign said, but it didn't matter. Her good mood made her want to help someone, and here God had put this man in her path. But what to do? Disturbing the big man might not be in her best interest, but if she knew anything from her past experience with both men and children, food went a long way. Money could be spent on things that didn't help the body, but food? It warmed the belly and the spirit both.

She turned towards the blinking light of the next door fast food restaurant. Unwillingly her mind flashed back to the times when Stacy would disappear for days at a time. How many times had it been her daughter on a bench outside some store? Wouldn't she have wanted someone to help her.

With a new resolve, she headed towards the smell of burgers and fries, returning in no time with a large sack. The man seemed to be stirring. Raising a muscled arm to his face to look at a watch strapped there. Taking the opportunity, she stepped towards him.

"Hello. I brought you some food in case you were hungry."

"What--?" The man seemed groggy from sleep, or something else, she couldn't tell, but as he pulled himself upright and she saw how big he was, the thought crossed her mind that maybe this wasn't the smartest thing she ever did.

She pasted the smile on her face. "Here you go." Fear warred with her sense on generosity, she thrust the bag into his hands and backed away. "Enjoy." She whirled, heading into the fuel station like she had first intended.

"Wait, Lady." the gruff voice called out behind her,. "I think you got the wrong guy."

All semblance of courage left her, she bolted towards the doors and the checkout where King stood looking around. The sliding of the door cut off anything else the man might have said.

"There you are! I thought you were headed in while I filled up."

Heart racing, breath coming in short little whooshes, Jill couldn't manage any words. Side stepping she managed to put King between her and the glass window. Peering around the tall cowboy, she got a peek of the biker type man squinting through the doors. He turned with a shrug and started digging through the fast food bag.

"Jill?"

She sighed and grinned up at her partner. "Just had an extra stop to make before I came in."

King frowned down as through trying to figure out if she had a secret agenda and she couldn't help smiling.

"I was just helping out stranded guy sleeping the bench out there."

King's hat lifted swiftly towards the door. "You did what?"

"I went next door and got a burger and fries. He'll be set for a few hours. Maybe he has friends coming, or gets a ride to the next town."

"You talked to him?"

She looked down at her feet. "No. Not exactly. He was sleeping on the bench. He had a sign on his chest. You know one of those like 'Will Work for Food' or 'Need a Ride to Nashville'."

The cashier cleared her throat and King stepped up to the counter. "Is that what it said?"

She checked the door. The man seemed to have

wandered back to his bench. "I don't know. I couldn't read it. I just popped next door, got one of the super meals, and gave it to him."

Taking his receipt, King steered her towards the door. She pulled back. "Let's go out this door over here. He's awfully big."

Unable to hide his smile, he shrugged. "Sure thing."

***

King opened Jill's door, all the while turning his head looking for her vagrant. The only man not fueling was a biker on a tricked out motorcycle eating a fast food burger. He lowered himself into the Jetta. *What would this woman be up to next?*

CHAPTER TWENTY TWO

"King?"

The cowboy woke from his slouch against the passenger window. "What's the matter?"

She'd debated about waking him the last ten miles, as cars seemed to desert this normally heavily traveled stretch of Hwy 55. Clouds hung massive, growing thicker and darker with each mile. In the distance blue gray fingers of rain reached from cloud to tree line.

"This weather seems really weird." The car in front of the Jetta jerked to the right and took a short cut to the frontage road across the ditch.

Jill stared after it. "What's going on with him?"

She fiddled with the radio, trying to find a local station. Maybe someone could tell her about an accident ahead.

After the smoke in New Mexico, the trip had been smooth sailing. King had stopped late every night at a cheap, but fairly clean, hotel where they each paid for a room and bid each other a soft goodnight. She loved every minute of it, but of all, the time side by side with King was the best. Sometimes silence would be the only thing between them, but it was never awkward. She had plenty of time to catch up on her Bible reading, and would sometimes read to King. He never said a word against it. At one stop she bout a tiny audio book, a Louis L'Amour about the Sacketts. She smiled every time Jubal's name came up, thinking about how she had first envisioned King as that character. The cowboy beside her sensed her humor, but never asked her about it. She suspected he knew it wasn't the story that amused her so.

But there was no humor in this situation. The sky heaved restlessly. Bulbous clouds formed brooding troll faces then backed off to flatten out, all in rapid succession. To the East, rain fell in thick sheets, highlighted by the hazy firelight of an afternoon sun.

King took one look at the sky then sat up and turned on his phone.

Tink. She jumped as something hard hit the window.

The man's eyes jerked up. "What was that?"

She shook her head. "Rock?"

Tink. Tink, tinkity tink, tink.

Hail crashed from the sky, obscuring the road. She slowed to a crawl. Brake lights flashed. Traffic ground to a halt. The ice lasted just a minute, then cleared, leaving Jill staring at the hood of the Jetta that now looked as though a herd of goats had used it as a bridge. She turned to King. His eyes remained on the sky. Despite the sudden calm after the hail, the clouds twisted as though unseen hands kneaded them from above.

Jill's knuckles tightened on the wheel, white in the gloom. Should she go forward? Stay here? More cars abandoned the interstate, some speeding past in the left lane, others cutting through the cars parked on the shoulder for the side roads.

"My weather app says a bad storm's on the way. The area's under a tornado watch. Says it's been bad already this year with 13 touchdowns in Indiana alone."

Jill gritted her teeth. "That's not helping, King."

He nodded slowly. "Sorry. What do you say about finding some cover?"

"I'm with you, but where?" Jill hated how her voice squeaked. She needed to stay calm.

King tore his eyes from the heavy clouds. "There's an exit in about a mile. We can make it."

A finger-like cloud protrusion pointed at earth. Jill tried to swallow around a mouth gone dry. "Okay." The traffic jerked forward, taking advantage of the clearing to make some progress towards safety. Cars clogged the shoulder, stacking under an overpass.

"Need me to drive?"

A car came up fast from behind, obviously not

seeing the flashing brake lights of the few cars inching forward. Jill tapped the brake pedal, hoping to get the other driver's attention. At the last moment, when she thought the other car would ram the Jetta, it jerked to the side and headed for a side road. Jill forced herself to breathe.

She gripped the wheel. "I can do this. It'd take more time if we stopped anyway." She stepped on the gas to follow the lights exiting ahead. A glance in the rear view made her pull over again.

"What is it?" King demanded. "Something in the road."

"There's a family in the car that got stuck. We have to help them."

King twisted in his seat. Jill turned with him. The car that had almost clipped her sat unmoving, rim deep in mud. A young lady jumped out and flung open the back door. She took out an infant carrier. Eyes wide, she scanned the surrounding cars as though as looking for help. Those cars that had been on the shoulder had moved on in the lull of weather, and those that saw the girl waving her free arm to attract attention, did not stop. Jill leaned forward, studying the sky.

"Back up." King said.

"Here?"

"Here."

The road was nearly deserted by now, so she put the car in reverse and backed along the shoulder. King leaped out before the car stopped completely and hurried towards the young woman.

Please, Lord, her heart whispered. A plea for safety.

The dead calm ended with a roar. The wind whipped along the highway, ripping at the woman's jacket. It snatched the blanket from the carrier. It spun high, snagging on a tree. King reached the little family. He took the baby carrier from the trembling girl and herded her to the car. Jill turned back to the front.

Like a massive, clay hand, fingers speared downward, grasping at the earth. Her heart thudded. They needed to get out of here. The back door opened, hinges protesting as the wind caught at it and flung it back. King helped the girl in and scooted the baby carrier next to her. He flung himself into the passenger seat.

"Get us out of here!"

She stomped the accelerator. Grass and gravel spewed from the tires, ricocheting off the guard rail. She ignored them. One eye on the road, the other on the cloud. The fingers disappeared and relief surged, then another appeared. Emotions jerked like a yo-yo. She drove, aiming for the exit.

King pointed. "There." She pulled off and slammed on the brakes. A pile up at the end of the exit ramp had cars stopped again. She studied the clouds. Growing up here she'd seen this type of sky and they rarely threatened. Something big was coming.

"We have to get to shelter," she whispered. At her words, the clouds made up their mind. Hail shattered down on the car like a thousand bullets. The girl in the back screamed and crouched over her baby, sobbing. Through the veil of white, Jill got glimpses of people abandoning their vehicles.

Fleeing towards the buildings of a strip mall just a hundred feet away. Could they make it? She looked at King. He seemed to come to the same conclusion. He twisted in the seat.

"Ma'am," he addressed the hysterical girl, yelling to be heard over the hail. "We've got to get to those buildings."

The girl shook her head. "No, no. My baby."

Jill put her hand on King's arm. "Wait."

He nodded. The cloud was invisible with the hail, but it lasted only seconds longer. The calm returned abruptly, unveiling a monster of a whirling cloud spinning several miles away. It tore at the earth like an enraged bull, debris flying in great clouds as the twister kissed the ground.

King opened his door. "We have to go. Now."

He flung the back door opened and grabbed the screaming girl. Jill ran around the side and reached for the carrier. The girl's eyes widened as she saw the beast bearing down on them. She grabbed at King. He half dragged, half carried her towards the safety of the buildings. Jill followed. One eye on the twister, the other on her footing. No way would she fall with this baby. She risked a glance down at a black haired cherub with wide brown eyes.

"You just hold on there," she whispered.

Hands plucked at her elbow and she looked up to find people reaching for her from the door of a gas station.

"Everyone to the back," a loud voice boomed. A tall man in a red shirt embroidered with 'Dave' waved people towards the rear of the store. "There's a cinder block storage room in the back."

Yes, but for how many? Jill was too short to see how many people were crushed into this little store, but a wave of bodies pressed towards the back, moved her. The air felt close and heavy. Her nose touched the back of the man in front of her. The knit polo nearly made her sneeze. *That's not King.* She jerked her gaze upwards, trying to catch sight of the tall cowboy. No luck. Bodies hemmed her in from all sides. Feet shuffled as they pressed towards safety. The baby whimpered. She rocked the carrier, banging someone behind her.

"Sorry," she murmured, glancing back. The man's wide eyed face pressed close. He tried to move her bodily towards the rear room. The wind whipped. Windows rattled.

Someone screamed. "My baby, I've lost my baby." *The girl.*

Jill rose to her tiptoes. "Here. By the candy. He's safe."

People pressed harder, but a small swath opened. King pushed his way through, sheltering the young woman with his arms as people tried to block them from coming to her. Jill reached out and pulled the girl close, handing her the carrier. The girl sobbed, trembling fingers fumbling to unbuckle the baby. Jill patted her shoulder, knowing the fear that drove her to try and hold her little one.

"I'd leave him in there," King advised. "He won't get jostled." Jill's eyes met his over the bowed head of the brown haired girl, knowing what he left unsaid. If the building took a direct hit, just maybe the protective seat would give the baby a little more of a chance. The building grew dark, the clouds outside turning day to night. A woman moaned in fear.

A scattering of lights illuminated the store with a painful flash. The crackle of lightening made her jump. King glanced outside and briefly a touch of envy bit her as he looked over heads.

"Transformer," he informed her from his advantageous height. For a briefest moment a smile touched his lips, as though he found her standing on her tip toes funny. The shaking of the girl crouched over her baby brought her back down to her knees. She rubbed the younger woman's shoulder, crooning nonsensical noises. The wind left the windows and thundered across the roof. Everyone ducked lower as something heavy banged across the top.

The world became that small dark space. Jill's vision narrowed to the press of bodies. The strangling smell of body odor. She closed her eyes. For a moment the only sounds were heavy breathing and whimpers. Her head cleared as she became aware of the strong chest of the man at her back, the tickle of the girl's breath on her arm. She leaned into King, drawing on his strength. *What do I have to fear?* She had the peace of understanding death was merely the next step, a sleep, then a peek at the Lord's glorious face.

Her lips moved in prayer. She offered up her heart to the Lord. *Forgive me for my fear, Lord. I know no matter what, Your plans are beyond my knowledge.* She was ready to go home.

The walls of the gas station dropped away and arms of peace surrounded her, cradling her like a child. The feeling was familiar. In that instant, she knew that these were the arms that once carried her that ten feet to the back door when her house burned. Arms of safety and love. At that moment, she knew without a doubt that Jesus answered. He was real. He was here. A tear tickled her cheek and nestled in the dark hair of the girl. In a rush the tiny gas station returned, the wind and the roaring, but she did not fear.

The girl nestled closer, bringing the baby within their combined embrace. "I heard you saying something." Her voice was tiny, just a thread under the wailing outside. "You were praying weren't you?"

"I asked the Lord to be with us." She whispered back, trying to find a more comfortable position against a rack of potato chips, her legs cramping from crouching so long. *Oh, I hate getting old.* Then she laughed at the thought, could be she wouldn't get much older. She leaned back and felt softness. King had made himself comfortable behind her while she had been lost in her own little world pulling her closer under his arm and against his chest. She fit perfectly. Embarrassed, she pulled away, but he shook his head. "It's alright."

The wind rose with a shriek, battering the glass door. The girl whimpered again.

"Shhhh."

"He's here." Her dark eyes stared at the candy just inches from her nose. "I felt Him when you prayed.   I'm   not   afraid   anymore."

Jill smiled. "You shouldn't be. He is here." As though sensing their peace the storm intensified and the dreaded sound of a train rose on the air.

"Get back here." King called to the manager. Manager Dave, standing by the door and peering out, dove away as the newspaper vendor from outside shattered the glass. He scurried on his hands and knees over dully glinting shards to join their little group.

"Get down." He called out. "Here it comes, and it's a big one."

CHAPTER TWENTY THREE

King leaned over and gripped the smiling woman in his arms tighter. *Crazy woman, always finding one reason or another to grin.* He tried to shield her, the girl, and the baby all at once. The baby took that opportunity to finish his perusal of the interesting faces and new place and let out a howl that rivaled the sound of the storm. More debris struck at the window, but none broke through and he tightened his arms, wishing he could do more. The store front rattled.

"I should have locked it," Dave muttered.

"Wouldn't have helped." King said. As though

to prove his words, the wind ripped the door from its hinges. Women screamed and men yelled. The woman in his arms sat peacefully. From his view he could see her cheeks curved into a smile. The hand stroking the girl's hair didn't even tremble. Though he pretended he couldn't hear their conversation over the wind, the edges of her words struck at him like knives. Her lack of fear proved her belief the Lord was in this ho-dunk gas station, and by her lack of fear, he could tell she believed it. The storm sucked at the opening like a straw, drawing racks against it until it once again closed. The rest of the cinder block structure quaked, but held.

The clear notes of a hymn rose above the moans. "A mighty fortress is our God," Jill sang, her sweet voice so reminiscent of his faithful mother that tears pricked at his eyes.

He gazed around him, fearful of what the other bodies pressed around them might feel. But with her singing a peace settled over the crowd. One voice then another rose. A biker, head and shoulders above the others, filled the space with a deep voice.

His partner, neck with scrolled tattoos and a deep red bandana, added her own words in an incredible soprano. A older laborer joined in, his Jersey accent adding more flavor. A young woman in fatigues harmonized.

As though leading a choir, Jill swung into 'What A friend We have in Jesus'. Voices rose above the howl of the storm. His chest swelled with pride. The wind rose higher, like Satan throwing a temper tantrum against the faith in the tiny gas station.

King turned his eyes to the paneled ceiling. He knew the sounds of a twister. Texas was rife with them. Once in his youth he worked as a storm watcher, warning those in the rural areas with sirens and horn to take cover. This one was a monster and if they took a direct hit, this little building and all the singing faithful in it would be gone like so much smoke on the breeze. Dirt filled the air, he dipped his face to his shirt to take a clean breath, but the singers never stopped. Stronger the voices grew. Swelling like waves. Challenging the storm.

He stared down at the velvety brown hair, streaked with red and tiny strands of gray. Thoughts of the past week crowded through his brain. What a ray of sunshine she'd become, not just to him, but to everyone. And here, in just a moment, she could be gone. His heart railed against the unfairness of it. Did she not know that a monster stalked this tiny store? She sang harder. No, it wasn't that she didn't know. She didn't care.

His anger raged against God, for the loss of Waylon, Carol, and maybe this little one here. He didn't care if he died. He should have been gone long ago with all the things he'd done. Maybe even secretly tried to kill himself with the alcohol. But no, he lived, while others died around him, swept out of his life in a flash flood of agony while he lived through it all. It wasn't fair. He nearly laughed at himself. How often had Waylon said that, and he'd replied life wasn't fair. But maybe, maybe, he could bargain. Him for her.

"Let her live," he prayed from the pit of his soul. "Let her live. If someone must die, let it be me. Let her live to be the sunshine in people's life. They need her." He gripped her arms tightly and she glanced up at him in askance. He couldn't speak, his heart too full. What right did he have to ask this of God. His sins ran deep and wide. A car, pushed by the wind, bumped against the glass, trying to force its way through the low cinder wall. A shudder racked through him, as he surrendered his life. Louder than a hundred packs of coyotes, the storm beat out it tattoo of fury one last time–then with ear ringing suddenness, it was gone.

King, Dave, and several other men rose and walked to the window. Feet shuffled through broken glass and scattered inventory. King pushed open the door and stood, watching the last of a dark finger disappear upwards, leaving nothing but an overcast sky.

He surveyed the damage from the doorway, knowing in his head it could have been so much worse. For the briefest moment he thought to pass the storm off as a hard blow rather than a tornado. But he couldn't lie to himself. Another man might have thought his prayer had come too soon. Foolishly thinking a bargain with God could change the path or force of a killer storm. But he had heard its blood lust, its hunger, all left unsatisfied as the Lord placed his hand over the gas station and the singing faithful.

He knew with every muscle, every fiber of his heart, that he should not be standing here. Cars sat at awkward angles. Roofs showed damage. But as people emerged, wide-eyed as though amazed they still lived, a peace warmed him from the inside out.

Jill moved to stand beside him. "Wow," she breathed. "I've never seen anything like this, not up close."

King nodded, his heart too full to speak yet. The feeling of being spared lingered, a chill of conviction of his sin warring with the peace given by the acceptance of God of his soul.

Her soft hand touched his. "Are you alright?"

He nodded, letting her fingers twine with his. The softness of touch, he barely remembered the feel. Like a starved man reaching for bread, he closed his fingers, reveling in it. As though her sunshine could transmit it's self, a warmth spread from her little hand, up his arm and straight to his heart. The dead shriveled thing, so recently lightened with the love of God, thumped back to life. A jerking, halting beat, but one all the same.

Jill looked down at their hands, the way he hung onto hers like a lifeline, and she squeezed it back. So glad that he was here with her.

A shaft of sunlight cut through the clouds, illuminating the broken glass throughout the parking lot and road like a sea of glass. The girl came to stand on his other side, the baby carrier slung in the crook of her arm with the ease of someone used to its bulky weight. The baby, exhausted from his cry, lay sleeping.

"Thank-you. For everything," she said. "I need to call my mom. She's probably worried sick." She fumbled for her phone. Seemed like everyone else in the store had the same thought, those that hadn't been recording through the storm, and screens lit up and voices murmured.

Jill stared off towards the interstate. "How do you think the car fared?" She chuckled. "You did get the extra insurance didn't you?"

He nodded, finding his voice at last. "Of course."

He stepped off the sidewalk, but did not release her hand, and led her out into the cool crispness that rode the shirttails of the storm. The Jetta's blue roof glinted dimly, battered where it had taken a hit from something almost as large as itself. But at least it was where Jill had stopped it and not in some store front like the red Volkswagen in front of him. It waited where they had abandoned it at the top of the ramp. Sirens wailed as emergency vehicles forced their way onto the roads. But over all the damage was minimal.

***

"Help. Oh, God. Help me!" A voice called from the pile up that had forced them to abandon the car in the first place. King let go of Jill's hand and trotted over to see what he could do to help. Immediately she missed the warmth and then chided herself for wanting him to keep holding it. *Again, you've only known him a week. Get a grip already.* But there he went, a knight in shining armor, being the hero again. An answer to someone's desperate prayer. In her heart she couldn't deny how much she admired the tall cowboy, and maybe even wished that he would let her get to know him better. And here she thought that with the wreckage of a storm around her. What was wrong with her? Acting like some moony teenager.

An ambulance and fire truck zigzagged through roads that were fairly clear. Jill went over to see where King was. He sat with his arm through the broken window of a car trapped between two other. A young man, face bloodied from flying glass, gripped his hands tightly.

"Just hold on there, Son, help's on the way."

The man sat pressed up close to his steering wheel, a deflated airbag in his lap and a lavender and blue bruise forming across a skewed nose. "I can't feel anything."

"You're in shock," King said. "Everything's there as far as I can see. You'll be just fine."

Then he completely shocked Jill by grasping those trembling bloodied fingers in his own large warm hands and bowing his head. His prayer was so soft only the boy could hear it, but the kid relaxed, tears seeping down his battered cheeks. "Bless you." he whispered. "Thank-you. Could you call my brother? My phone is in my shirt pocket. Let him know I'm okay. "

King leaned forward to comply.

He's hatless, Jill realized with a start, her heart thumping so hard it threatened to suffocate her. He had prayed with the young man, this cowboy who was so bitter he blamed God for the loss of his son and ex-wife. Some where, at some time, the Lord had worked on his heart. Her hand, the one that he had held so tightly, curled and she pulled it close to her chest. His heart had softened and he had let go of that anger he'd used to build walls around him. Already the difference showed. A new man knelt by the car.

The ambulance crew finally made it to the wreck and took over King's place, but not before he was able to place the call for the young man and tell the brother where the kid was.

He straightened and turned back to where Jill waited near the Jetta. The smile he gave her, so like his old one, but still so different, shot straight to her heart. She knew in that instant that she loved this man.

CHAPTER TWENTY FOUR

Jill swung the Jetta's door shut and gazed around the yard. "Boy, it's good to be home."

King hefted his pack from the hatchback and slung it over his shoulder. He eyed the modular guard shack with sagging panels and the main office of cinder blocks and gave her a dubious look. His eyes lit on the shiny white dodge sitting under a security light within easy view of the the watchmen. "Sure is."

If he'd been anyone else, she might have thought he disagreed with her, but in the past week she'd come to recognize his quiet humor, and when he was serious. This might be a transitory home for her, and his might be in the truck, however this place already had the feeling of home. A place both familiar and exciting. In the office, a paycheck waited and another load headed to who knew where.

The knowledge that she would be going off alone hit her like that air bag had hit that kid. King had held her hand through this first run, but no more. He drove in a different division and would be going his own way. The cheery thoughts that had buoyed her spirits as the car pulled into the gravel covered yard dissipated like clouds in a Texas summer sky.

Just a short week they'd been through so much, she come to admire the tall cowboy. She didn't want him to go. She didn't want to say goodbye for now and see each other in passing. She bit her lip, chastising that whiny part of her. This is what truck drivers did, the life she'd chosen.

As though sensing the direction of her thoughts, King held out his hand. "It's been a pleasure, Ma'am. I guess I'll be seeing you." Then, just like that, he turned and left her standing by the little blue car. Such a cold leaving after everything. Had this trip only been special to her? She wanted to call out to him, to ask if she imagined everything, if that spark she felt for him was in any way returned. He strode to his dually without a backward glance, opened the door and started unpacking. Would he call her? Should she call him? No one beside Sam ever seemed to communicate with him. Would he mind if she reached out?

"Bye," she said belatedly.

He hadn't even waited for her response, most likely eager to get away from her. A week in close quarters with anyone was hard, especially a virtual stranger. Most likely he needed to get some breathing room. After the Cadillac Ranch visit she had felt comfortable in his presence though, allowing for the quiet times—so she had slept a good portion of the way back—without the awkwardness that fell between people who didn't know each other well. They both aired their demons and agreed to disagree on God. So why hightail it so fast?

She shook her head. It shouldn't matter. She wasn't here to get involved with the first man to run cross country with her. She finally turned to the office. Time to get moving, earn that first paycheck, and put the images and thoughts on the long legged cowboy out of her mind.

"There you are!" Stu waved at her from the steps of the office. "I'd thought you disappeared off the face of the earth. Are you ready for another go?"

Jill tried not to cringe. She had forgotten that she'd sort of promised they could do a haul together. She glanced back at King. He had stopped digging in his truck and watched the greeting with his usual bland expression. Did she imagine it, or did the lines around his eyes tighten?

Ashamed she'd looked at him, she forced a smile on her face and headed into the office. "Sorry about that."

"You could have called," Stu's voice had the slightest bit of whine to it that reminded her of a petulant child. She leveled her best mom gaze at him, she hated whining and wasn't about to let someone start with her.

"I guess I didn't think about it."

Stu's face seemed to drop some of its friendliness for a quick second, then he pushed up close to her in the narrow hall and tried to pluck her backpack from her shoulder. "Here, I'll take that for you."

She held on tight. "That's okay. I've got it."

"It looks pretty heavy for a little lady, let me take it for a spell."

No way would she let the other drivers see someone else carrying her bags. And she definitely didn't like the way 'lady' rolled from his mouth. Besides, she needed to appear confident and competent, not let someone do things for her. A moment later she decided it was a good call when she stepped into the driver's room and found it filled with drivers of both genders, all turning to take a look at her and Stu framed in the entrance. For the second time in just the few minutes since she'd left him, she missed the cowboy and his quiet mannerisms. Compared to the gentlemanly way King conducted himself, Stu's pushiness felt like running her hand over broken glass.

She almost turned and bolted back the way she'd come, hunt down that white Dodge and tell him how she felt, shake him and force him to believe what a blessing he was to her. But she didn't, all she managed was a longing look past Stu to the door, praying that King would regret the unspoken words between them and appear. But he didn't.

***

King kicked the tire after Jill disappeared into the office. *You're such a lily livered coward. Say something. Call her back. Make her understand how much this trip had changed your life.* Tell her you don't want her to go. He'd face anything, even that tornado again But he didn't. He opened his mouth and the words stuck to his tongue.

He stared at the shadow on the uneven ground, the wings of the handmade boots jutting from his legs, arms akimbo and hat low on a face lost in the the shadow. That was him alright, a shadow of a man, unable to tell a woman how much she meant to him. He might have found forgiveness from God, but it was so much harder to change himself. To embrace the idea that he had worth after so many years spent wallowing in despair. Even then, did he have anything to offer her?

This was his life. He was a trucker. She was a driver.

He smacked his palm onto the railing of the truck bed, then slammed the back door, grimacing as it bounced off his foam mattress cover and clipped his shin. A passing driver gave him a wary look and then a wide berth. King obliged him with a sneer then stopped himself. The softer feelings inspired by the tiny woman nearly giving way to the habitual nastiness. But he was beyond that now. He was a new man in Christ.

He had to go in there. Drop off his paper work. Do laundry. Do something. But he didn't want to see her after fudging their goodbye.

Besides, the way she taken off with Stu got under his skin like a chigger. He eyed the other man's white Ford. Thoughts involving a knife and tires flitted through his mind. Then, as a surprise to him (and anyone else who might have seen him), he barred his teeth in the parody of a smile.

Immediately his mind turned to Jill. No, she might not have agreed with his evil turn of thought, but she did teach him to see the humor in the smallest thing. Shaking his head in disgust at how fast and how thoroughly that little ray of sunshine had infused his life, he shut the door more carefully this time and then hopped behind the wheel.

No, he wouldn't go chase after her like some darn fool. She'd think him a stalker for sure. Poor thing didn't need that worry on top of all her others. He ran his finger over his phone and stared at the office, wishing she would walk back out the door, give him a chance to start his goodbye all over again. And if she did, what would he really do? Glare at her while Stu hovered over her shoulder? His phone turned green and he swiped through his contacts until he found her number and the head shot he snapped of her sometimes during the trip. Despite the uncertainty of the situation, her smile was courageous, her eyes glinted with curiosity.

He slid his thumb over the keypad, trying to find the words. Only goobly gook highlighted the screen so he tossed the phone onto the center console. Snatching his hat from the clip where he'd just placed it, he headed towards the office.

Still no Jill. Most likely she had plenty to do. She had mentioned she wanted to check on Marion again. A tinge of jealously colored his vision for a minute and then he let loose with a heart felt guffaw. Here he was, acting like a love sick coyote. She probably hadn't even given him a second thought, wrote him off as a helplessly twisted man. Even as he thought it, he knew Jill never wrote anyone off, even the daughter that had tried to kill her. For her sake he prayed that her penchant for giving second chances didn't get her hurt again.

As the word 'prayed' crossed his mind, he froze. The word rolled around in his head. He hadn't hoped or wished, no, he'd prayed. It'd come so easily too. His hands turned to ice—sweat trickled down his back. It was for Jill, nothing more, for her he would pray to the God he had cut himself off from when He'd allowed his little boy to die in some forsaken wilderness. His mind skittered away from other such dangerous thoughts and he picked up the phone, a smile curving under his mustache. He knew just what to say.

CHAPTER TWENTY FIVE

Jill's phone beeped with a text message, but she didn't check it with Stu hovering. The long haired man behind her gave her a slight push so he could get into the driver's room. The sour smell of unwashed bodies and microwave food hit her in the face and she nearly gagged after the taste of the clear air of the highway.

She wanted to turn around again, but Stu flourished a hand. "Hey everyone, this is Jill."

She flushed, hating to be the center of attention. One or two drivers turned from the company computers on the back wall. Two women looked up from their microwave dinners.

A man pulled down a newspaper. "Stuff it, Stu."

She studied the women from under her lashes, curious about any other women drivers. She'd not seen any. Not that she'd had the chance, but she'd like to make their acquaintance. Pick their brains on thoughts about working for this company. How long had they been at it? How they did deal with men like the one at her shoulder? She thought about figuring out a way to ditch the hovering man so she could talk with them, but she had other things to do.

Jill headed towards the pay window with her paperwork. The bespectacled woman on the other side gave her a friendly smile. At her elbow burned a red candle. Jill leaned forward to try and catch the scent through the speaking hole. Cinnamon, one of her favorites. The woman's smile grew as though she knew Jill needed to escape the other room's smell and she couldn't help but grin back.

Stu plucked at her shoulder. Her annoyance returned. "Why don't you stow your stuff? I'll watch it while you do your errands."

"That's okay. I've got it."

The pay secretary swung her chair over to take the envelope through the slit at the bottom of the glass. Good thing she had filled it out in the car and didn't have to do it under Stu's prying eyes.

"Good afternoon, I'm Becky. I don't think we've met."

Jill couldn't help returning the smile. "Hi, I—"

"This is Jill, Beck. I've told you about her." Stu laid a heavy hand on her shoulder—again. "We're going to take a load here as soon as Sam can get us a trailer and a drive away going the same way."

The other woman's smile wavered, but her blue eyes stayed steady on Jill, eerily so, as though she were trying to tell her something. As though speaking to the secretary reminded him he needed to bug Sam for a load, Stu stalked off down the hall towards the dispatchers, raising his voice to warn Sam what he wanted—or else.

For the first time since walking into the building, she relaxed. Becky swung away to put her envelope in a pile of about ten others. Jill took the opportunity to pull her phone from her pocket and slide her finger to check the text before Stu could return.

She smiled as King's scowl appeared. He hadn't wanted her to take it, but even in the small picture she could see the way his eyes sparked. It was obvious not many people wanted his picture, even though he was the one that insisted they needed each other's numbers. Glancing around to make sure the other driver was no where near, she tapped the message.

"You're the blessing. Thank-you."

Her lips curled though tears pricked her eyes.

A soft hand reached through the small window and touched hers. "You okay?"

She smiled up at the concerned face of the other woman. "Just a text from King."

Becky frowned. "It'll get easier. The new will wear off and they'll start to leave you alone. If King gives you any trouble, though, you tell Sam. For some reason he knows how to straighten that man out."

Jill shook her head. "King's no trouble. He's wonderful." She bit her lip at how easily that slipped out. Her eyes slid down the hall, hoping Stu hadn't heard. Anger quickly followed his thought.

The office worker stayed silent for a moment, as though trying to overcome her shock at someone besides Sam defending King. Well, she better get used to it because Jill was tired of people warning and worrying about her around him. Stu's voice raised floated down the hall. He was the problem. Not her cowboy.

"—any of them." Becky continued.

Jill studied the other woman, "I'm sorry, I didn't catch that."

"Don't let any of them push you around, especially that one." She opened her mouth as though to continue, but Stu appeared at the end of the hall.

"Got it all lined up, Sweets."

Jill gritted her teeth.

"It's off to Joplin and it's not UPS trucks for us. You have a sweet little Selaro. Of course, I have a class A since I have a CDL, but don't worry, Toots, you'll get there."

Jill tuned him out and started down the hall, then stopped and whirled back. "My name isn't Toots or Sweets, or any other nonsense. You may call me Jill or my handle."

Stu frowned at her show of defiance then seemed to make an effort to smile. "Okay then, Jilllll. You finally figured out a handle. That's good." He leaned an elbow on the counter of the pay window and winked at Becky. The other woman kept her expression blank. "So what do we call you."

"Sunshine." She spat and then turned on her heel to go check with Sam about this load Stu supposedly secured for her. Stu's chortles followed her down the hall.

She paused at the doorway of Sam's office, regretting her out burst. Now that she thought about it she didn't want anyone but King calling her Sunshine. The way he said it in his deep rolling voice sent shivers down her spine and made her smile every time. Stu's lips wrapped around the same word just made her shudder.

"Come on in, Jill," Sam called.

She flushed, realizing that she had been standing in front of his door simmering for almost half a minute.

She started to take a step in when Marion burst out of his own cubicle. He reached out a hand. "Jill. I thought I heard your voice. You didn't get caught in those terrible storms over West did you?"

Jill let him fold her hand in his big ones, studying his face. It didn't have the flush that may have signaled the high alcohol levels of a functioning alcoholic. His eyes were bright and clear, he seemed to be brimming with news.

"We did get into a big blow on interstate 55 but we were able to pull over and get out of it," she answered.

Sam motioned out his small window. "Is that your Jetta out there?"

"King's. I hitched a ride back with him." Did she just blush at the mention of the tall cowboy?

She caught the two men sharing a look over her head. The heat climbed higher.

Marion moved to the window and whistled. "Looks like someone took a baseball to it."

Thankful for the distraction, she nodded. "It was pretty scary there for a while, but the Lord held his hand over us. King and I took shelter in a convenience store. The storm ripped the doors off, but besides a few fender benders, it wasn't too bad. King took the wheel after that and got us out just fine." She just had to throw her partner's name in there every chance she could, didn't she? Sam's watchful eyes studied her as though weighing each word.

Mentioning God brought Marion's head around and he approached her again. "I'm glad you made it back safe. I never did tell you thank you—for praying with me that day. I went home to some great news. Kelsey's doctor's appointment went better than expected. They think they got it all."

"That's wonderful news."

Marion nodded at Sam and headed back to his

own office. Jill collapsed onto a chair with a big sigh. Sam studied her across his desk. "You okay?"

"Yes, just in awe at how God works in people's lives. If I'm too close to see Him in my own, I just have to look outward and see Him in everyone else's."

"Amen." A comfortable silence fell between them, the only sound Stu's voice echoed down to the small office.

"Stu seemed to indicate you were ready for another load."

She straightened. "I am."

"With him?"

She shrugged. "I guess. He said there were two, and they weren't UPSs."

Sam looked down at his desk to hide his grimace. "No UPSs for you. It's a nice little unit, a short jaunt. I think you'll like it."

Stu's laughter rose over the lower murmurs of talk. Jill couldn't help cringing.

"You okay with this? You're sure?"

She would not wimp out on a load just because

her partner couldn't be King. He himself had said that traveling with people when you were drive-away was just good sense. "Yes." She made the single word firm.

Instead of seeming relieved, Sam frowned. "Alright, here's your trip information. But just like before, if you need anything, you call me. Okay?"

She took the manila envelope. "Okay."

Chapter Twenty Six

King fisted his hands against his thighs, watching out Sam's office window as Jill prepared to jump into her unit. She paused and looked around one last time as though searching for someone before climbing in and following Stu's motor home out the gate. Had she been looking for him?

His goodbye had been so awkward when he wanted to say so much more. To say thank you for reminding him of God's love, for bringing peace and sunshine back into his life. To ask her to stay. But who was he kidding? He had nothing to offer her.

"So that's it then?" asked Sam's voice from

behind him.

King turned from the window and looked at his friend as he swiveled back and forth in his office chair. "What do you mean?"

"You're just going to let her take off?"

King shrugged. "Not much I can do. She works here. It's her job."

Sam kept his gaze steady as though trying to make him understand something. But for what? "Do you just lie to me, or do you got yourself convinced she doesn't mean anything to you?"

A blaze of surprise tore up King's throat, nearly choking off his air. But this was his best friend here. The one who had seen him through thick and thin, at his best and his worst. "Am I that obvious?"

Sam shrugged. "Only to me. But right away I could see the difference in you, Bud. Especially when you look at Jill. You need her, King. You need each other."

"I'm no good for her, Sam. I'm no good for anyone. Never was. Never could be."

"That's the old King talking. I know that God

brought you both here together at this company at this time for a reason. You've both got things in your past. Everyone does. But God gives second chances, King, and this one is yours. Don't waste it."

King turned back to the window. The yard seemed emptier some how, his world bleaker. What would happen if he jumped in his truck and chased her down right now? Told her he needed her after just six days. She'd think he was crazy. And after everything he'd revealed to her he had to be the last person in the world she would want. Look how fast she'd gotten another load with someone else. She'd put the pedal to the floor to get away from the yard as fast as she could.

Behind him Sam's silence grew. The other man's gaze burned holes in the back of King's light cotton shirt. He removed his hat and ran his hands through his hair.

"I just can't, Sam."

For a long time his friend didn't answer, then the rustling of papers reached his ears. "I have a travel trailer going down to Joplin."

King groaned. *Did no one respect a man's wishes any more?*

"Man, you're getting picky. It's a light load, good pay, medium mileage. What more could you want?"

"One not headed the same way as Jill and Stu maybe."

"Picky, picky, picky." Sam muttered under his breath. He clicked a few computer keys.

"Nope. I'm tellin' you it's the best one we've got. Don't you trust me?"

King didn't turn from the window. "Nope."

"So you're going to take it then?"

"Sure, put me on it." He could go get his phone and get on the board on his own. May was a busy month, there would be plenty of loads. Still, he let Sam assign him like a newbie. *What's going through that pea-brain of yours, King?* Did he think he'd catch up with her? Run with her again? Stu's smirk flashed before his eyes. His hands fisted again. It would feel so good to wipe that expression off of his face.

He sighed. *Forgive me, Lord.* Already losing control, but he honestly couldn't stand that man.

Behind him Sam clicked away, unaware of the struggle inside his friend. "There. It's yours."

"Thanks."

Sam cleared his throat. "I'll keep in touch with her for you."

King headed for the door.

Sam was just as bad as he was? One of them had to face the facts. He had nothing to offer the woman. He wouldn't bring her down if he failed at life again. No, best to keep his distance.

"Don't bother."

***

Jill paused before climbing into the Mercedes Selaro. *What are you waiting for, silly? Do you think he's going to run after you like some happy ever after movie?* Besides, now was not the time for love, she had too many complications in her life as it was. King could be a big one of those. How would he feel about her ducking and running every time her daughter called? How would he feel when he learned that his Sunshine was nothing but a hypocrite? Instead of letting God take control, instead of trusting His wisdom and praying about her situation, she ran. No this was better.

Pulling out of the yard felt like ripping her heart out of her chest. King made her feel safe. Her heart might beat like a thousand drums when he was near, but it wasn't from fear of him, never from fear. She didn't get that same feeling around Stu. In fact, if he kept it up she'd have to straighten him out. Always leaning over her, putting his hand on her arm to steer her around like she couldn't walk on her own. His grip tight. Almost possessive. She couldn't help but to compare it to King's gentlemanly ways. His strong but gentle hands. Disturbed by the unkind thoughts of Stu she shifted in her seat.

To distract herself she clicked on her blue tooth and called Shawn.

"Hi Mom. What'cha doing?"

"Driving. I'm trying out this handy new toy

King suggested. I just have to say who to call and I can talk to you without fiddling with it." Why did it hurt to say his name? She needed to get a grip.

"That's great. Welcome to the 21st century."

"Ha ha."

"So where are you off to now?"

"Joplin."

"Are you still traveling with King?" Okay, they both needed to quit talking about him.

"No. I have a new partner. Stu." Shawn was silent for a minute.

"Oh."

"Oh? What does that mean?"

"Nothing. Just from what you said about him, King sounded like a neat guy. I just felt safe with you running with him. What's this other guy like?"

"He's okay." Something in her voice must have cued Shawn into her edginess around her new partner.

"Okay?"

"He's just different than King, not as. . ." How to put it nicely after all the dark thoughts about the other driver. How could she describe how something just felt off with Stu, forced, when with King it seemed so right and comfortable. ". . .quiet."

Shawn let the words hang in the air. "From what you said King seemed like a nice guy. I'm surprised you aren't doing another run with him."

Shrugging though he couldn't see, she glared at the trailer in front of her. "Well, he is in a different division. This other guy, he talks—a lot."

Her boy's laugh filled the cab and she smiled right along with him. "He's not the one that made you change your number is it?"

Sore subject. "No, that was Stacy." For some reason saying her daughter's name just didn't seem as difficult as before. Maybe her talks with King had helped, he'd said they would. She tuned back to the conversation to find Shawn had changed the subject to talking shop. She let the words rush over her, happy that he was happy, but not understanding much as engineering jargon interspersed with other things over her head filled the cab.

"I'm glad you like your new job." She added

when he came to a break. "I'm at the company's affiliate station. I will get back to you later."

After hanging up and pulling into the fuel aisle, Jill found she had to brace herself for another few minutes in Stu's presence. Hopefully, it would be a fill and go. It struck her as amazing how she already missed King. It certainly looked like this would be a long trip, despite the fact it wasn't even half the miles of her first.

CHAPTER TWENTY SEVEN

Stu sat busy at one of the booths, papers and logbook spread over half the table at the greasy spoon outside of Joplin. She hesitated a moment. She honestly didn't want to sit with him, her dislike growing with every word out of his mouth. This was not a good start to the trip. She definitely could not imagine trapped in a car for any amount of time. She sighed, but she didn't want to alienate anyone either.

She slid into the booth opposite him. "Do you mind if I sit?"

An expression of anger flashed across his face as he pulled the papers towards him and shuffled.

His reaction surprised her and made her more curious. "Go ahead."

She looked across to where he tapped a pen across two log books he'd stacked together. "Catching up on your logs?"

He nodded. "You can say that."

"Don't let me interrupt you. I should do that as well. King told me to keep them up every time I stopped."

At the mention of King's name Stu's face grew tight. "That man can be a self righteous prick. If you want to make money with this company you need to keep two log books."

"Two log books? How? Is that legal?"

Stu shrugged. "D.O.T gets tougher every year. Most people keep two. That way you never run out of hours."

"That seems like a lot of work."

"Maybe. But it's all fiction anyway." Now that she knew what he was doing, he pulled out the logs and started working on them again. "I'll show you how if you want."

A shiver ran up Jill's spine. It just felt wrong. "That's okay. I think I'm good."

"It okay for King to show you stuff then, but not me?" he snarled.

Jill sat back. "Umm, well, he's not here, but I don't think I need shown. It doesn't seem right to have two log books. What would you turn in?"

"The one with the most hours obviously."

She didn't like his tone at all. It reminded her of her ex-husband's jealous rants when she was out of his sight for more than an hour or two. She made furrows in the grease on her plate. Shifting uncomfortably against the broken vinyl. Of all the places she had stopped with King not a one had been as bad and run down as this. She fiddled with the necklace, a smile touching her lips as she thought of the other man.

A clatter of Stu's plate on the table announced the arrival of the waitress. She eyed Jill. "Anything wrong with the food?"

"No. I guess I'm not as hungry as I thought."

The waitress jerked a shoulder and trudged on.

Jill wiped at a spot on the counter. "Do you stop here much?"

Stu didn't look up. "Doesn't matter where I stop, I can't tell one greasy spoon from another."

"So you don't care about the parking or anything?" Was she needling him on? Maybe. But then again, maybe she needed to find something, anything, to like in the man. So far she'd come up with zip. An uncomfortable itch started in between her shoulder blades.

Stu's head jerked up at her last remark. "I don't care as long as I can get in and out. King tell you something about me?"

"Oh no, not about you. Just to be on the lookout for good places to stop because getting in is often easier than getting out."

The other driver smacked his fork on the table. "That little tale teller."

Inching back in the booth, she studied her partner. "What?"

"One time, and I mean one time only, I get stuck under a height bar, everyone's gotta make a big deal out of it. This company is bunch old biddies with their gossip and tale telling. King even suggested that they put it in the training manual. Know your parking and what not."

Jill hid a smile. That *was* one of King's favorite phrases alright. "Oh. King didn't say anything about you having an accident."

Stu snapped his logs shut. "Sure he didn't."

Did he just call me a liar? Obviously he was touchy about his accident, but his reaction seemed way over the top. She hadn't even known about it. Her heart jerked, something about this conversation didn't feel right. The happy, jovial man seemed to be changing before her eyes. Closing her eyes for the briefest second, she offered a prayer for patience, peace, and safety from above.

Opening her eyes she found Stu regarding her strangely. "What were you doing?"

The way he asked set her teeth on edge. "Just saying a quick prayer over the food. It looks like it could use it." She dropped her eyes at her lie and added a prayer that the meal didn't give her food poisoning.

"Well stop it," Stu's eyes darted left then right. "People are staring."

A quick glance at the other diners revealed, just like any other place, people immersed in their own lives. Not a one met her searching gaze.

"I'm sorry that it made you uncomfortable, but I often pray. I like talking to God about things."

Stu started shoveling his food into his mouth. "Well, don't do it around me, I don't like it. I can't believe King didn't break you of that. He usually pipes right about those sort of things. It's about the only thing we agree on. Let me finish and then we can get started."

She bit back the retort that King was a lot more tolerant than people thought, but the following words made her head snap up. "What do you mean? I thought we were parked for the night."

The tall man gave her a greasy smile that nearly turned her stomach. "You know what I mean."

Spooked now, Jill pushed her food away and stood. "I'm sure I don't know what you're talking about. I'm headed in."

Stu tossed his napkin down on his plate. "Food stinks anyway. I'm coming."

She shook her head. She definitely didn't want any more of his company. "No."

Ignoring her, he threw a couple of bills on the table then turned and pushed on the back of her arm, subtly forcing her toward the door. Her skin cooled where he touched her and she pulled her arm closer to her side, trying to get him to let go. He didn't get it. Not wanting to make a scene, she let him guide her, but once out the doors she jerked her arm from his grasp.

"Let go of me and don't grab me again."

Stu's eyes widened then narrowed in anger.

Jill took a breath. "Please." she added belatedly.

"What kind of game are you playing here?" He leaned towards her as though to take her arm again. She stepped out of the way.

"I don't know what you mean. I'm not playing a game, but I certainly don't like to be grabbed or pushed."

Stu advanced closer. He didn't grab her but she retreated until the wall of the diner stopped her. She tried to move around. He put one hand on the wall blocking her. She went out the other side. He stopped her there too.

"Now, let's talk about this attitude of yours a minute."

"My attitude?" She couldn't follow the conversation. Her attitude wasn't the problem.

He nodded. "Here I am, showing you the ropes, teaching you about log books—"

"I didn't ask to be shown log books, especially something illegal."

He put a hand on her lips. "Let me talk. You always got to be talking."

Jill looked towards the door, hoping that someone would come out. But it was late, the patrons at the diner comfortable, and the lights above the side where she was cornered flickered, leaving them half in shadow.

"I think you owe me something, don't you? I

even bought you lunch."

"You did?"

"You know, our first date during training."

Date? "I don't owe you anything," she said as firmly as she could. She put a hand on his arm and pushed. He didn't budge. "I can reimburse you for the lunch if that will help. And it wasn't a date."

He grinned at her. How could she have ever thought him nice? Eyes like black holes leered down as his face drew closer. "It won't help. But you could give me a kiss. That might make me feel better." Understanding flooded her. She pushed on his arm hard, finally getting away.

"Absolutely not. I don't know where you would have gotten such an idea." She fought to keep the trembling from her voice. Her heart beat thunder loud in her ears, her blood roared through her veins. Where did she find men like this? *Oh yeah, 'hit the road' I said, 'It would be fun' I said.* Perhaps she hadn't fully considered the dangers.

He leaned against the wall, arms crossed, unconcerned with the outrage in her voice.

"Where'd I get the idea? You spent a whole week with King. We all know you hooked up with him."

A flush climbed her cheeks. Quick memories of the feeling of her hand in King's, her wish that he was the one God had set aside for her flashed through her mind. Even in the dim light Stu must have seen it and saw it affirmation of guilt.

"There you go. Already forgetting about him aren't you? Easy to do when you come with a real man. Sam should have given you to me in the first place."

Rage filled her, both at the unjust accusation of both her and King's character', but also that Stu thought himself in any way close to the man that King was.

"You're nothing like him," she shook her finger at him. "He's kind and good and would never think of insinuating the things that you are. You stay away from me, you hear." He had said we. How many employees had gossiped behind her back about her and King. Sam and Marion hadn't shown anything by their interactions with her. Was Stu making it up? It seemed he liked to misconstrue things—like her relationship with King?

She hadn't realized she still had her hand out, shaking with rage. Stu grabbed her arm and pulled her close, dipped to kiss her. She twisted away. His lips slid across her cheek. She stumbled and retched and stomped on his sandal. He released her in surprise and she stepped back. Where was the door? She needed to get back to the diner. She'd stay all night in there if she had to. First she needed to make it clear that she didn't ever want to see this man's face again.

"Don't come near me again, Stu. I will be delivering on my own in the morning. Before or after you, I don't care, but I don't ever want you near me again."

Stu stepped forward as though to make a grab at her. Spinning away, she trotted towards the door. Her phone trilled. Trembling fingers fumbled at the button. If worse came to worse she could have whoever was on the line call the police.

She pushed into the anteroom of the diner.

"Hello?"

"You'll be sorry!" Stu yelled behind her.

"Mom? Who is that? What's going on?"

"Shawn. Thank you for calling. It's just some guy." She collapsed on a seat for waiting customers, wobbly legs unable to hold her up any more.

"It sounds like you've been crying. Are you okay?"

"I am now. It's just-" Should she tell him? Her son had been through so much. She made all the wrong decisions when it came to men. Oh why, oh why couldn't they all be like King? "A driver thought I owed him something is all. It's okay now, I asked him to leave me alone. I'm going to stay here in the diner for a while."

"That doesn't sound like a good situation, Mom, are you sure you're okay?"

"Yes." She tried to sound confident for him, but then again, their history together, he'd seen her at her worst. He'd seen her cry. He suspected something wasn't right at all. And there was no way she could keep it from him. "Don't worry about me,

Shawn. I have it handled—"

"Did he yell 'you'll be sorry'?"

So he'd heard that.

"Yes," she peered out the glass door, no sign of Stu. "He's gone now. I told him I would be delivering on my own—"

"Mom—"

"—I'm just thirty minutes or so from my delivery."

"Mom—"

"—The trip was a good one, easy, just one day. I love this freedom." The words came in a rush, trying to convince her and him both, but they fell flat. Ringing false before they even left her mouth.

"Mom! Stop! This sounds like a dangerous situation. Are people around? Are you being safe?"

She grinned despite herself. "I'm okay, Shawn. Really. I am in a diner right now." *But what happens when it closes?* "I'll make sure I walk with someone to the motor home."

"This isn't good, Mom. I worried about this."

After the stress of Stu her temper flared. "Don't

you start in on me how this isn't safe or anything." Not him on top of her parents and sisters. Could no one understand? She closed her eyes and took a deep breath. Maybe they couldn't. Did she really? Why hadn't she stayed put and trusted God to take care of her? Why was she out here on the road? Alone. With a man who had just threatened her?

She peered out the window, straining to see her motor home. Stu's unit was gone. Relief washed through her. Rough wood scratched at her back as she sank onto the warped bench.

"He's gone."

"Are you sure?"

"His motor home isn't there."

"He might have moved it."

"That's okay. As long as he isn't around. I don't care."

"Maybe you should call that other driver you went with last time."

"King? Why?"

"Just the way you talked about him it seemed like he knew how to handle things."

"He's long gone on a load of his own, Shawn. Drivers from Sea2Sea go across the U.S., even Canada."

"You could still call him."

"I—I don't want to bug him. He's kind of private."

"You mean you haven't tried to talk to him at all?"

She wanted to. So much she'd reached for her phone many times in this short trip. "No. Why?"

"I don't know. I just thought he seemed special to you is all." If only he knew. But perhaps he did. Her son was very intuitive about things, especially when it came to her. Maybe she'd leaned on him too much over the years, first with her husbands and then with the mess with Stacy. She worried him. She forced confidence in her voice. "I'm going to head out, now. Spend the night and get delivered in the morning."

Shawn's silence stretched.

"What?" she demanded.

"You should call him—King."

"No." She snapped. He hadn't tried to call her at all. If he felt anything like she did, he would have right? But he didn't, so she needed to move on. She gotten too attached to the man in too short of time, the feelings that she'd developed for him had been girlish, more like a crush really, and obviously weren't reciprocated. "I'm going now. I'll call you in the morning. I need to get some sleep."

"Mom—"

"Enough Shawn. Everything's okay. Thanks for calling. I love you." She hung up before he could get another word in. She loved the boy, but she wasn't ready to talk about King, nor her anger at him for not calling. If only it had been him here with her, she'd never be in this situation. Why hadn't he called her?

She chuckled at herself. It was her decisions that put her here. She couldn't go blaming him. Yes, he'd left, but she'd gone off with Stu immediately. Had she even given him a chance? She closed her eyes. *Lord, forgive my foolishness. I just can't seem to learn from my mistakes.*

CHAPTER TWENTY EIGHT

"Ma'am?"

The gruff waitress from earlier peered from a half open inner door. The lights had been dimmed. The smell of pine cleaner seared her nostrils. Time had passed too quickly-it must be early in the morning now. "Yes?"

"We're getting ready to close."

That late already? How had she missed people walking out the door right next to her? She offered the other woman a smile, but only got a glare in return.

"Okay. Are you headed out any time soon?"

The woman's face softened. "In a few minutes."

"Do you mind if I walk with you?"

"The manager doesn't like for anyone to be in the diner after closing time."

"I could wait outside."

The other woman nodded. "Okay. I"m parked out back, but I'll give you a lift to your car."

She touched the woman's arm. "Bless you."

The waitress covered her hand with her own. Hard calluses scratched at Jill's knuckles, belying the softness of the back under her own palm. "It's that man you were with, isn't it?"

Jill nodded, unable to speak past the lump in her throat.

"That guy's bad business. He's been here a time or two over the years. Enough for me to watch out for the younger girls."

***

How did everyone else seem to suspect Stu's true character? She'd been so blind. It made her miss King all the more. He seemed to be able to see so much in people. Even if he were blind when it came to her. She didn't want to admit that it the more likely problem was that her feelings weren't returned. But the way he called her his sunshine— even now it brought a smile to her lips and a peace to her heart. She ran her hand over her phone, wanting to call him, but why couldn't he call her first? She didn't want to drive him crazy.

Slipping out of the diner, she hugged the side of the building. At any moment expecting Stu to jump out of the shadow and make a grab for her.

He didn't.

She peered across the street to the all night gas station. Was King there? Had he taken one of the other loads to Joplin? She leaned against a newspaper dispenser. She thought maybe she saw Stu's trailer over in the fuel aisle. No sign of the shiny white truck and the tall cowboy driver. She slumped. She didn't want to be anywhere near Stu. Best to hit the road and get to her delivery tonight, maybe there would be space to wait until they opened. She shook her head at King's admonition to know her parking. Here she was, breaking his well intentioned rules already. Then again, she never should have gone with Stu. It was obvious King didn't like him. *Why, oh why, didn't you trust him?*

A maroon car pulled in front of her and she jumped. It was just the waitress come to pick her up as she'd said. Thankfully Jill slipped into the dark interior.

"Thank you for doing this," she breathed. "I guess I'm just being silly."

The waitress shook her head. "Never feel foolish for being safe. We ladies have to stick together, you know."

Jill studied her profile in the dim light. Older, just like her. What had this woman seen and done over the years that made her so protective of the 'girls' at the diner? Jill was glad those other waitresses had someone like this. At first impression she seemed hard, but her actions spoke differently. A lot like King in fact.

"I'm that motor home over at the end of the lot."

The waitress clucked. "Try to park closer next

time, and under a light."

Jill nodded, refusing to take offense to the woman's bossy tone. Not after Stu had manhandled her.

"And don't stay the night here. Move over to the travel center where there's more people. This parking lot has become a place for drug dealers and others because it's so dark. Last year there was a murder."

A shiver ran up Jill's arms. "Thank you for doing this."

"No problem. Use your head and don't get yourself in situations like this."

Jill opened her door and paused. "I don't even know your name."

"Evelyn. Yours?"

Jill smiled. "Jill. Thank you again and again. You're an angel."

The woman chuckled, a pleasant sound that scratched at her throat as though she didn't do it too often. "You be careful, Dear. God be with you."

Jill jumped out and into the safety of the motor

home. Thankful Evelyn stayed until she had locked the doors behind her.

***

King adjusted his phone so that it aligned edge for edge with the place mat of the all night restaurant near Joplin. It was hundredth time he did it since he had left the yard, checking the screen to see if his Sunshine had texted or called, making sure it was never far from his hand.

She never did.

He sipped at the coffee, straight up black like he liked it, and then he smiled thinking of Jill's preference for sugary drinks. Sweet, like her. He nearly groaned at the sappy thought.

Admit it, King, you've got it worse than a tom turkey. Not only did he had feelings for her, she hadn't called. Obviously those feelings weren't returned.

He stared out the window. Red and orange lights whisked by, merging into a steady stream. He tried to see the individual vehicles, ignoring the smaller cars, and looking for those lights that would indicate a motor home. Was she out there? Passing him now? He didn't know how Stu traveled. Would he push her. She shouldn't be driving this late. She might get tired. Fall asleep at the wheel and run off the road. Why that snake, he'd . . . He relaxed his hands from around the coffee cup and touched the phone again. *Maybe just a short text to check up on her. What if she's getting sleepy?*

Surely she'd call him if she was tired. He'd talk to her. He shook his head, he'd made it clear he didn't chit chat. Not with anyone. Anyone that was except her. He bowed his head. *God look after her, please.*

This whole trip an uneasiness had set up shop in his soul. A spur sharp feeling that he should have interfered with her leaving with Stu. Jealousy? Straight shootin' it was, but something else nagged at him. The way Stu touched her. The annoyance in Jill's every movement. The look she gave him when they parted, as though she'd wanted to say something and he hadn't given her a chance. *You're such a fool, King, always were. Taking God up on his grace for a second chance didn't cure stupid.*

He pulled the atlas close and ran his finger along his route. It should be the same as Jill's, and if the other two drivers kept it legal and didn't push too hard—two hours ahead tops. Granted, he'd pushed harder than he should, but sleep hadn't come easily. This is why he sat alone in the diner, staring out the window. Praying Jill would call. Wishing he had the strength to call her.

What would she think if she found he was on the same route? Would she think him the stalker type? After knowing her fear over her daughter finding her and her past with abusive men, he didn't want to give her that impression at all, but darn it, the woman trusted to readily for her own good. It was a wonder she'd made it this far—and that had been only by the grace of God.

IIe recognized now that God had a plan, both for him and her, and he prayed that it was for them to be together. He snorted, a worn out truck driver with a shady past wasn't what she needed in her life, but he sure needed her. His life felt empty without her warmth, not hollow and worthless like before he had turned back to God, but as though something were missing. He knew it was her.

He jumped when his phone rang, sloshing coffee a little too close to the key pad. He grabbed a napkin, answering before the second ring without checking the screen—only a few people had his number, Jill being one of them.

"'ello?"

"King?"

He pulled the phone from his ear and looked at the numbers—not one of his contacts. "Yes?"

"This is Shawn, Jill Mason's son."

King crumpled the napkin. "What is it? Is she okay?"

"I don't know. She called me acting all funny. The guy she was with threatened her while I was on the phone with her." Anger curled King's fingers into fists. The instinct to pound Stu into a dung beetle ball warred with reason.

"Where is she?"

"Joplin. She didn't say where exactly."

"That's okay. I'll find her." He slid his phone shut and closed his eyes. He prayed for strength and speed before making another call. He didn't care that it was the middle of the night. The boy had already rousted Sam out of bed to get his phone number, so he'd be wide awake to get the earful King had planned.

CHAPTER TWENTY NINE

Jill couldn't sleep. She sat in the front seat of the motor home, eying the trucks around her. She had moved across the street to the more lighted parking lot, but each time an engine started or a truck pulled out, she jumped. Checking the doors, ready at any minute to see Stu pounding on the window. Finally, she could take it no longer. Better to get going than spend a sleepless night seeing monsters behind every truck. The delivery was only 20 miles away. She honestly didn't think Stu waited somewhere in the dark, but by taking the back roads she could avoid the most obvious route. Just in case.

With a plan of action she pulled out her atlas and began mapping her route. It would take her a few miles out of the way, but the map seemed to indicate plenty of frontage roads running along side the interstate. It would be no problem to keep her bearings. So near three o'clock in the morning she started her unit and hit the road.

For a while everything seemed to go well, she found the back road with no problem and followed it.

The wee hours of the morning were a peaceful time to drive. The adrenaline still gave her caffeine-like jitters, but this was the perfect end. She'd just get to the delivery before Stu did and get out of there. Hopefully there would be a place to park for a few hours. She cringed when she thought of what King would say about her lack of research into a place shc'd bccn going. However, thinking of the cowboy in the tall boots made her smile. He would be proud that she checked for low bridge warnings on these roads.

Just as she began to congratulate herself, the

motor home jerked. A fine sweat broke out on her lip. *Teach you to get overconfident*. The engine purred on again. She relaxed the death grip on the wheel. King had told her sometimes bad gas could be the cause of rough going. The motor home sputtered. *It's going to die.*

She managed to get herself on the shoulder, thanking God that it was wide and paved, before it died with a final jerk. *Feels like I'm out of gas.* She tapped the gauge. Nope. Full. Plenty of fuel for this short trip. She turned the key. The engine whined back. She slapped her palms on the wheel and sat back.

"Great, just great, Jill. Can you possibly get yourself into any more trouble?" She fingered her phone, wanting so badly to call King. Instead she called the yard.

"'ello?"

The kid on the other end of the line sounded half asleep.

She tried to keep her voice cheery. "Hi, this is Jill Mason, driver number 1564, I'm calling in a breakdown."

"Ma'am, it's the middle of the night. No one's on duty." Exactly what King said when the last truck had a flat tire.

"But I'm stranded in the middle of no where and—"

The voice on the other end of the line sighed. "Alright, alright. I'll see what I can do. You drivers are all the same. Expecting people to hop to every time your unit has a hiccup."

"Thank-you. I appreciate it."

She closed the phone and sat in the dark and quiet, breathing deep to keep away her fears. What if Stu followed her? She glanced in the mirror. No lights. The road deserted.

She fingered the phone again, just itching to call King. She fingered back through the history, looking at the texts Shawn had sent her, reading the messages of encouragement. Such a good kid. Her eyes froze on a text she didn't remember seeing.

> **Shawn:** Hey Mom, here's Stacy's number
> if you get the urge.

When had he sent that? Two days ago? Three? Did it matter? Would she ever use it?

She laughed at herself. Sitting here on a deserted road, could it get scarier? As if with a will of their own, her fingers dialed her daughter's number.

***

The bright lights crested the hill about a mile down the road. Jill rubbed her arms, mind wandering, a smile in her heart. Stacy had not been perturbed by the early morning phone call, in fact had welcomed it. After all the crying on both sides, they had agreed to meet. If she ever got out of this new mess.

So far the approaching lights were the first in over a half hour. Fear chased goose bumps up her arm. The roar of multiple engines rattled the windows. The noise rose, reverberating through the floorboards.

She hung her head out the window. As the sun pinked the horizon, a flock of motorcycles in V formation blocked the bird songs that should fill the soft morning air.

A prayer touched her lips. A wish that King was here.

It was a moment before she realized the sounds had ceased, one at a time like a chorus of crickets in reverse, the engines cut. A glance at the side view mirror showed the whole flock parked behind her on the wide shoulder, a tall man in dark leathers kicked his stand down and stood while the others in her view seemed to relax on their bikes.

She forced herself to breathe as the man approached the driver's side. Should she slink down and crawl to the back? Pretend that someone had turned on the flashers and left to go find help? The man approached, kicking the tires as he came up the side.

He looked up and caught her reflection in the mirror and straightened, now approaching with purpose. She gulped and leaned back, stretching forward at the same time to flip down the locks. The sound was like a gun shot in the sudden quiet and the man's face lit up with a grin.

A knuckle rapped the window. Should she open it? She studied his face. Shadow of a beard. An American flag bandana. Odd. His face seemed familiar somehow. One of the man's brows cocked down as he studied her, as though she too jogged a memory.

Resigned to whatever fate God had in store for her, Jill cracked the window.

"Are you alright, Ma'am?"

Still mute she nodded.

"Can we give you a ride somewhere?"

"I—I have help on the way." She hoped the kid hadn't forgotten her and breakdown would be calling soon.

He nodded and stepped away as though realizing he frightened her. The man had to be halfway over six feet at least. She relaxed at his thoughtfulness. "Thank you for stopping, though, it was thoughtful."

"No problem." He shook his head. "I feel like I know you from somewhere, but—" He held up a finger. "Aha."

She couldn't help a smile and widened the crack. "What?"

"You're the crazy lady that gave me a meal at that truck stop a week or so ago. Where was I, Cuba?"

Heat climbed her cheeks. "That was you?"

"So it WAS you?"

"Well, I did give a man a meal—"

"That was me. I was sleeping on a bench waiting for the rest of the guard to show up for our next mission."

Jill blinked. Did he just say mission?

"And you came and gave me a bag of food."

"I thought—" How do you tell someone she thought he was a vagrant and needed food? Maybe not the wisest idea when he'd just stopped to help her.

He grinned as though he could see the thoughts in her head. "You thought I was a bum." He chuckled and straightened into his full height and saluted with a snap of leather. "Sergeant Charles Hagele of the Patriot Guard at your service,

Ma'am."

"Oh my goodness. You weren't a—a--a--"

"Bum?"

This time she opened the door and slipped to the ground. "I am so sorry about that." She stuck out her hand. "I'm Jill Mason. I hope I didn't insult you?"

"No Ma'am. A hot meal has never insulted me yet." He jerked a thumb over his shoulder. "The squad got a good kick out of it when they finally showed up."

"So you're on your way to a mission?"

"Nope. On the way back. You broke down?"

She sighed and motioned to the motor home. "I guess I am. I do have help on the way though. Breakdown should be opening up soon to get a tow truck out here." She added with a rush. Probably wouldn't do to let people know she was alone. Of course, the guard did out number her ten to one. Out here there was no one to hear her scream. She put a foot on the step. *Why did you jump out of the motor home so fast?*

"Mind if we take a look?"

His kind voice and easy manner again put her at her ease. He motioned to the front engine.

"Are you a mechanic?"

He grinned. "Nope. I'm an accountant." He raised his voice and hollered towards the other motorcyclists. Some had gotten off and were walking around stretching and talking in the early light, but no one else approached. Thoughtful of them.

"Hey, Paul. Come here a minute." Another dark leather clad man broke off from the others and headed up the length of shoulder.

"Chuck?"

"Lady's truck won't run. Can you give it a look?"

Paul shrugged. "Sure. Can you start it?"

Jill shook her head. "It died. I turned the key and it just goes rrr rrr rr."

The biker headed toward the front of the bus. "Give a try and let me hear it."

She climbed in and turned the key. Once again

the engine worked, but didn't turn over. Chuck propped himself against the door and watched the other patriot lean into the engine.

"Paul IS a mechanic. A good one too."

A half a second later, Paul's head appeared around the side of the engine. "Are you out of gas?"

Jill frowned. Was he insulting her because she was a woman? Then she relaxed a bit and laughed a little at herself. Here God had sent help and she let an innocent question get her riled. She *must* be tired. "No. I filled up at the last town."

Paul nodded at her and shifted his eyes to the man beside her. "Got a knife?"

"Sure." Chuck straightened and pulled a Swiss Army knife looking thing from his belt and flipped out a blade. Jill gulped. These men were armed. Then she brushed passed the fear, if they wanted to hurt her they'd have already done it right? There were enough of them they could kidnap her and the motor home and no one would be the wiser on this deserted stretch of road. Then it struck her. What in the world did he want with a knife? But now Paul and Chuck both were under the hood.

"Try it now." Came a voice, which one she couldn't tell.

She turned the key. For a moment the same thing happened, the growling of an unhappy engine. Then it rumbled to life with a happy shudder.

"You did it!"

Chuck closed the hood with a short drop, but the expression on the faces of both men were grim. The mechanic handed the knife back to Paul, but something else peeked out of his other hand. Before she could ask, her phone chimed. A text from King

> **King:** Coming up on a broken down motor home.

How did he know? The only people she had told were Shawn and breakdown.

She leaped out of the motor home and faced back the way she had come. Traffic had picked up now and cars whizzed by, seemingly curious of the gang on the side of the road, but too much in a hurry to stop, or even pull over into the other lane. Jill paid them no mind, watching for the glistening ivory truck and the purr of a diesel engine that signaled the arrival of her white knight.

King pulled up and jumped out of his truck nearly before it stopped moving. Her heart leaped as he strode towards her, his eyes checking her over as though to reassure himself she was okay, and then studying the two men that had followed her from the front of the motor home.

Oh how she had missed him. Even his scarey stern face didn't mar her joy. She knew it was all a hoax. The way he protected himself.

She jogged to meet him, wanting to allay his fears. He grabbed her shoulders when she got near enough and gave her a good look. "Are you okay? You had me worried. Why didn't you call? I was just across town."

Jill blinked up at him. "I didn't know where you were. You never even texted me after I saw you at the yard."

The cowboy nodded. "I'm sorry 'bout that. There was just too much to say that I couldn't figure out how to start. I kept meaning to but—" He hugged her tight to him again. "I'm glad you're safe."

The adrenaline of the evening before and the break down finally let loose of her limbs. Her legs trembled and she leaned on him, burying her face in his shirt as the sobs started. "Thank you," she whispered between hiccups. "Thank you for coming."

How could she tell him how much seeing him meant to her. Like her personal angel sent to rescue her yet again. She knew without a doubt that God's hand directed everything. Her giving Chuck the meal, him stopping to help her, and finally King being close enough to come. "Thank you for coming." Gulping in a breath she rushed to reassure him. "I'm fine. Just a little scared. There was an issue with Stu but—"

He pulled her into a tight hug, her face pressed against the cool cotton of his button down.

"King—can't breathe."

He loosened his hold, but didn't let her go. "I was going out of my mind for worry. Why'd you take off like that?"

"I just needed to get away—Wait. You know about Stu?"

He nodded. "Shawn called me."

"Shawn?" She felt like an idiot repeating his every word, but it seemed so circular. How did Shawn call King? How did he get the nerve to call a complete stranger when she couldn't bring herself to do it?

"I wish you had called me, Jill, I would have been here that much sooner. Why this road? The interstate's just over there."

She shrugged. "I just had to leave. I got to jumping at every sound. Forget about sleeping. I thought by taking the back roads I could avoid him, get to the delivery, and get out of there before him. I wish I had called you too." She bit her lip and looked up at him. "I wanted to, honestly, but I didn't want to bug you."

King laughed and pulled her into a hug. "You can bug me any time, Sunshine. Any time." He seemed different. Freer, happier.

She snuggled into his hug. "You should be proud of me, I even looked at the atlas for all the low bridges."

He nodded, his face turning grim. "But you broke down." He raised his gaze to the men behind her. "What if he had followed you, Jill?"

"I know. I wasn't thinking clearly. I thought I would put some miles between us, get as far away as I could."

King nodded and repeated his words. "But you broke down."

"I did. Isn't that odd for a new motor home? Two loads and two breakdowns. Not a good start I'm afraid."

He shrugged. "Nope."

But she could tell that his thoughts weren't focused on her any more—it was on the men watching, though they seemed embarrassed.

Jill motioned to them. "This is Paul and Chuck. They stopped when they saw me on the side of the road."

King shook each man's hand in turn, but still

kept an arm keeping her close. She snuggled into his warmth, thankful for another shoulder to share the worry.

"Did you say the lady had some trouble with someone?" Paul asked, sizing King up with his eyes. The men nearly stood the same height, though King was on the leaner side.

Her cowboy nodded curtly. "Last night."

A look passed between Paul and Chuck Jill didn't like. She knew without a doubt that it involved Stu somehow. Chuck held up a black zip tie. Then she remembered, when he had handed Paul back the knife there had been some else in his hand, something they wanted to talk to her about, but King had arrived and side tracked her.

"This was used to crimp the fuel line," Paul explained. "The vehicle would run a ways and then stop. It had worked loose somehow, that's why she was able to get this far."

Jill leaned onto King now, her legs barely able to hold her. "You mean, someone did that on purpose?"

Paul nodded. "Yes. And not too long ago either."

"Maybe it was done at the manufacturer," she tried. "Maybe they forgot to take it off for some reason."

Paul twisted the zip tie in his hand. "Where's that?"

"Indiana."

He shook his head. "No. This was likely done when you fueled at your last stop."

King took the piece of plastic from the other's hand and held it up to the dim light, nodding to no one in particular. He didn't seem surprised.

"You knew," she whispered.

King pulled back so he could look down at her. "I suspected."

"How? Why?" Oh goodness. She had not been imagining Stu's presence. Some how he had done this to her. But to what end? She shivered to think of it. Then anger rushed to replace it. *Why did he let me go with him if he thought he was that sort of man?* And she could tell by his frown he hid more with his silence.

***

King put the tie in his pocket and then looked at the other men. "Thank-you for stopping and helping her. It's good to know there's still good people on the road."

They shook hands again while Jill simmered.

Chuck gave her a grin. "Thanks for the hamburger, by the way."

She flushed, could she get anything right? Good thing he had a sense of humor about some strange lady thrusting food at him. Before she could say anything, King turned to her. "Why don't we get these vehicles somewhere safe so we can talk."

She nodded, still not trusting herself to speak. They'd talk alright, and she'd give him a piece of her mind.

CHAPTER THIRTY

The travel center seemed like home after half a night on a deserted stretch of road. By the time Jill parked, the trembling in her limbs had ceased and she began to reflect. She still did not appreciate being kept in the dark about the kind of man Stu was, but the fierceness of King's hug, the worry in his eyes had softened that tight knot of anger—just a little.

King met her as she hopped down from the motor home. "I don't think there's any place inside. Why don't we get a cup of coffee and talk out here."

She gritted her teeth. "I don't need a cup of

coffee."

The cowboy nodded, as though sensing her mood, and sighed. "You might not, but I do. I drove all night and now that I know you're safe I need a pick me up."

Again her anger softened. He had been so worried, she clutched at it again, but nodded. "I'll walk with you."

They walked in tense silence and filled Styrofoam cups from a pot of coffee that poured so thick it might have been sitting there since the time the station was founded. Jill added a lot of sugar, the let down from the worry and excitement of the night finally catching up with her too. She took a swallow, closing her eyes and forcing it down. Willing her shaky hands to steadiness.

She smiled when King took his own sip and grimaced. He must be tired, for he reached for the sugar packages. It was bad joe, she'd never seen him take it any way but black. He turned towards the door and she followed.

"You knew Stu might try something?"

"No Jill. I never thought he'd try to force anyone."

"But?"

"Your tire, that first flat you had back at the yard, was on the suspicious side."

Vaguely she remembered one of the repairmen and King looking at the tire. "Suspicious how?"

"Like it had been knifed."

"You knew?"

He held up his hands as though to fend her off and she realized that her whole body leaned towards him like she would bite his head off. She forced herself to start walking again. Spying some benches at the end of the parking lot, she headed that way.

"I said it was suspicious but there are so many things that can happen to a tire. I did talk to Sam about it."

"But why didn't you talk to me? It was my tire."

"I couldn't be sure."

"But you suspected?"

"Not until after we got back with that first load.

I didn't like the way Stu crowded you." He looked down into his coffee. "I guess I was a jealous some."

She ducked her head at his reference to his feelings, confusion about her own warring with her anger. He had dropped everything to come rescue her. Her relief could be described when she had seen him and had missed him when he was gone. She admired him so much. Could this gentle man who had been hurt in the past truly care for her? Did she care for him?

"I needed to talk to someone, so I talked to Sam. He said he'd heard some talk about Stu, but the women hadn't come right out and reported anything. But that every time he left the yard or tried to hone in on a woman he felt uncomfortable, like God prodding him that something wasn't right. That's why he insisted I take that first load with you. Especially when he noticed Stu taking an interest."

"Well, he could have warned me."

"Nothing to warn you about. Just rumors and suppositions. A jealous hunch. You just can't go accusing people of things" Like Stu had about King-funny, he'd been warning her against another man that he should have applied to himself.

What seemed to catch her attention most was his phrase 'a jealous hunch'. What did he mean by that? She stayed silent, her mind straying from Stu to the man beside her. The man whose arms had felt so good—so right. She turned towards the sunrise, wanting to believe, but afraid to ask. She'd made too many mistakes, always leaping before taking a good look at where she would land.

King seemed lost in his own thoughts, but his silence didn't last too long. He spun back to her. "Jill. I have to tell you. I know how you can't know. It's probably cheesy after just a short time, but I—" He stumbled, closed his eyes and took a deep breath. "I think I love you."

At his words, her heart leaped. Tears sprung to her eyes like a sudden spring shower. His words freed her heart to think the same back at him, but she couldn't say it. There was too much in her life, too much fear and uncertainty. Unresolved issues that hung over her head. How could she say she loved him back when she didn't feel free, not yet. Now more than ever she knew she had to finish this, to face her fears and her daughter so she could move on with her life.

King seemed to sense her reluctance. His eyes dropped. "I understand if you don't feel the same. I just needed to tell you." His mustache quirked to the side in that half smile she had come to love. "I didn't want you to think I was stalking you or anything." He shrugged. "I guess I was though, taking a load along the same path and—"

Jill touched his lips with her fingers. "It might sound cheesy, but you have made me the happiest woman in the world with those words. You're the kind of man I've dreamed about since I was a girl looking in all the wrong places."

King's eyes lifted to hers as she dropped her fingers to her side. "I sense a but in there somewhere."

"Not really a but, well I guess it is. I'm not free. I have to deal with Stacy. Problems from my past and I guess a new problem now that I feel are smothering me. Keeping me from moving on."

She waited for him to loose his temper, to pout, she even cringed back in her seat. There was no reason and she knew it.

Those storm cloud eyes gazed at her steadily. "Alright then. Let's do it."

"Let's?" She repeated

"Of course. You didn't think I'd leave you to take care of those things on your own, did you?" He gritted his teeth "Especially the Stu thing. I think we need to talk to Sam again."

"But you said there's no proof. Especially in the tire."

"No, you're right. But there's enough circumstantial evidence that he can be watched like an egg stealing snake from now on. The second something suspicious happens with anyone else he's going to be gone."

Jill nodded. "I called Stacy this morning."

He quirked an eyebrow. "You did?" She didn't have to look at him to hear the question of 'why didn't you call me then while you were beings so gabby?' in his voice.

"I'm supposed to meet with her when I get a load to Texas. She can't leave the state so I'll have to go down there."

He squeezed her hand. "I'm proud of you. That must have been a tough call."

She sighed and sank down to the bench. "It actually went very well. She cried. I cried. She asked me to try and forgive her."

"Will you? Can you?"

She nodded. "I think I can. I mean, look at what God has forgiven me. I spent years being scared and for no reason. If I had just trusted Him more, I wouldn't have run. I wouldn't be in this situation now. But my foolish fears make me do stupid things.

"Well, I'm glad you came to Sea2Sea. I wouldn't have met you otherwise, and I wouldn't have realized how badly I needed forgiven myself."

She stared, knowing she looked like one of those puffer fish, complete with bug eyes and open mouth, but she couldn't help it. This man surprised her every time she turned around. She couldn't help the joy that leaped through her heart.

"He found you and saved you didn't He?"

King nodded, the tightness of his hug never fading. "During the tornado. I wanted to tell you, there was just so much I didn't know what to say."

Could this man get any more perfect? Thank you God for sending him to me. "It doesn't matter. I know now. I should have known, I could tell. You were always a good man, but you prayed with that poor boy in the car and I suspected, but I didn't want to make you angry."

"Because I have a terrible temper?" He looked worried that she might be afraid of him like everyone else.

"No. I know how private you are about things —I didn't want to be prying into your personal affairs." She looked up through her lashes. "I know how that gets to you."

A chuckle rumbled through his chest and vibrated against her cheek like a purr. "You're a sassy thing, you know that?"

"I do. It' s gotten me into plenty of trouble."

"Yes. I can see that. You've shaken my life up something good."

"I didn't say I was trouble."

"Maybe that should be your handle."

"Hey. You called me sunshine. That's mine and I'm sticking to it."

"Okay then, Sunshine. Are you ready to hit the road and get this load delivered?" He pulled back and gazed into her eyes. "If you can't though we can always ask a favor Sam and get someone to pick it up."

"Hmmm, favors? I thought you didn't do favors."

He shook his head. "Doesn't matter. As long as I'm with you, who cares?"

Mention of Sam and favors, made Jill get to thinking. "How did you know where I was?"

"Shawn called me."

"What do you mean, Shawn called you? How?" That word seemed to keep leaping to her lips.

"He must have called the company and got a hold of Sam who sent him my way."

"How? It's the middle of the night?"

King smiled at her and tipped her jaw closed with a gentle finger. "You have people that care about you, you know. Sam always makes sure he has a point of contact with another member of the driver's family. Most likely he called Shawn while you were in training and exchanged numbers. Of course, then Sam gave Shawn my phone number."

"Sea2Sea seems to have a problem about doing that."

King nodded. "We'll have to talk to them about that too, I guess. But he explained that he'd told Sam he was worried about you and that you had mentioned you'd called me." Jill put a hand to her head, the world seemed to be spinning with all these round-a-bout connections. A tear escaped. How strange and mysterious indeed were God's ways.

"That's how you knew. That how you were so close."

"Yes. Shawn told me he was worried about

you. I knew a company guy who was at home not far from here. I called him and asked for a favor."

"You asked for a favor?" *Another? Did miracles never cease?* "How far did you go in debt tonight because of me?"

He nodded with a little laugh. "He owed me for picking up his load when he dropped his transmission in the middle of Interstate 55. Didn't make me any money, but I was in the area. Anyway, he came and got the trailer and I headed this way. Then you called and I put the pedal down, just hoping I was here on time." His eye searched her face. "He didn't. . .hurt you did he?"

Jill hid her face in her hands.

"Jill?"

She shook her head, too overcome to speak. He'd asked someone to take his load, her son had called him, she felt so loved and so blessed. A hand cupped her shoulder followed by an awkward pat.

"Blast this console."

She turned and laughed. "I'm okay. No he didn't hurt me. Just scared me."

As though sensing her laughter may be a jumping start into hysteria, King pulled her close. She melted into him. She felt so safe and protected when he was near. She lifted her face, gazing into his storm cloud eyes, waiting. She didn't have to wait long. He kissed her gently.

"You're safe now."

"I know. You always make me feel safe." She leaned back and couldn't help smiling at him. "I don't know why everyone's so afraid of you, though. You're really just a big softy."

He frowned. "I'm not perfect, Jill. I might be a new man in Christ, but I have a past I'm not proud of."

The stubble from a sleepless night poked her palm as she touched his cheek. It was a stretch, but she managed. "We all have pasts, King, but we are all new in Christ. What matters to me is what I see. You have always been kind and considerate, no matter how you tried to hide it. I have always loved that about you." She wasn't free, not yet, but she had to let this wonderful man know how she felt about him. It may be crazy, falling in love in so short a time, but she knew deep in her heart this was the man for her. "We may both have had long roads getting to each other, but I know you are the man God set aside for me."

With a smile as bright as the new sun bursting over the Missouri horizon, King squeezed her shoulders. "Thank-you."

She sighed, the feeling of being in his arms like coming home. She sent a quick thank-you to the Lord for this wonderful man and snuggled deeper into the safety of the hug.

CHAPTER THIRTY ONE

Jill faced the sandwich shop. Her heart slammed against her chest like a flat tire on the road. Her breath hitched. King's door slammed and his hand slid so comfortably into hers, giving her the strength to get control of her emotions before they slid into a full fledged panic attack. But then again, the episodes had miraculously disappeared as quickly as they had come. Long talks with her daughter, sometimes daily, had helped to get to know her child again. That, the quiet support of the cowboy at her side, and a renewed faith that God had it all under control, gave her a focus she had been missing.

Squeezing the long fingers, she squinted through the glare to where she was to see Stacy for the first time in ten years. The place looked clean and busy with a constant flow at the drive through and wide spaces for RVs. Jill couldn't help the smile that came with her assessment of the parking lot. Boy how three months on the road can change one's perspective of the simple things. Like how wide the lines were between parking spaces.

Realizing that she was procrastinating, she squared her shoulders and took a step towards the door. Maybe, just maybe, today she would truly get her daughter back. King didn't move with her. When she looked up into his hat's shadow, he quirked his mustache and raised his free hand to point left.

"Mom?"

Jill turned. A car sat parked under the branching crepe myrtle not too far from King's big truck.

"Shawn!" She rushed to her son and hugged

him. "What are you doing here?"

"I—" Shawn's eyes raised to King's. The other man set a hand on her shoulder, giving her a squeeze. "I didn't want you alone when you did this."

Jill looked up at King, heart full to bursting. He said he'd help her do this and he had. He'd made it easy to meet up with Stacy face to face. He had arranged the loads to Texas. He'd called Shawn. He understood how important this was for her to move on with her life.

She patted his hand. "Thank-you."

"Anything for you, Sunshine."

Her cowboy leaned forward to shake Shawn's hand. The mistrust in her son's eyes seemed to fade as he studied the man before him. Of course, they had talked on the phone since that early morning call when King had gone to help his mother, but this was the first meeting. Jill hoped, and could tell, that he liked what he saw. King was so different from the other men in her life. She had always been attracted to the wrong sorts, maybe deep down hoping she could save them. But King loved the Lord just as much as she did, and he stood by her side in all things.

She faced the sandwich shop resolutely. "Shall we do this?"

Another squeeze on her shoulder told her the man beside her was with her 100 percent. "I'll wait in the truck."

She caught at his arm. "Oh no, you don't." With her eyes she begged him to stay.

He nodded. "If you're sure. I don't want to be in the way."

He looked at Shawn and her son nodded. "Love to have you. It's just lunch."

Entering her daughter's new place of work was one of the hardest things Jill had ever done. Although Shawn's promises that Stacy had changed still rang in her ears, she had insisted that they meet at this public place in Houston. This was a major mile stone for her daughter, her first job in her new life just a bike ride from her new place of residence. It was plenty far away from the small Texas town where her old friends lived and where she had tried to kill her mother.

Jill let her eyes adjust to the bright yellow walls, and tried to pick her daughter out of the crowd of milling workers behind the counter. Could she after all these years?

An anxious faced turned towards the door at it's simple chime. The curve of her cheek, the auburn hair, these were things that a mother could never forget. She had kissed that head, tapped that nose.

Stacy's face bloomed into smiles. She stepped from behind the counter, wiping her hands on a towel. Jill thought she'd be frozen in fear at seeing her daughter, like the phone calls had sent her into panic attacks. But there was a softness in her daughter's face she'd never had before, and anxiousness about her welcome that tugged at Jill's heart. She stepped towards her daughter and the next moment wrapped her arms around her waist.

Stacy sobbed on her shoulder. "Oh, Mom, thank-you for coming. Thank-you. Thank-you. I'm so sorry."

"Shhhh."

"I've wanted to tell you forever, I couldn't get through—"

King's warm hand on her back gently guided the gaggle to a booth in the back. Her daughter clung and sobbed. She held her tight. The bands around her heart finally letting loose and flying free as the floodgates burst with forgiveness.

"'It's okay." She caught Shawn's eye. He stood close on her left, obviously feeling like a third wheel. She reached for him and pulled her family close, rocking her grown children as though they were babies. So what if the other patrons glared or smirked. Her family was together for the first time in too long. She smiled at King across the table.

God had given her the strength to face this, and He gave her a man who would stay at her side forever, further strengthening her. Although she made up her mind to come see Stacy while stranded on the road, she didn't know if she truly would have gone through with it if traveling with King hadn't bolstered her confidence in the rightness of her decision. He had never pushed her. He'd simply made it easy to get two loads to Houston, one drive-away, one tow-away, and after a couple phone calls with Shawn here they sat.

Heart full she kissed the sweet heads of her children, so thankful to have them back.

Shawn sat back, wiping his eyes with quick movements. Stacy stayed close, arms around her mother. She stared at the man across from them.

"Shawn told me about you—you must be King."

Jill couldn't help it, she tensed, but nothing in Stacy's voice that hinted at spite or anger—those emotions she used to live with constantly. All that reached Jill's ears was curiosity.

He nodded. "King Loveless, nice to meet you."

"Loveless?" She slanted a look at her mother and hid a smile. Jill used to call him Loveless Leader, but she didn't any more. He was her beloved and he showed her such love, the name no longer fit.

"King and I plan to get married," she said. Both

sets of her children's eyes swung her way. She looked down where Stacy's hand clasped her own. "We were just waiting on—" Her voice drifted off. She didn't want Stacy to feel any worse than she obviously did.

"Me." Her daughter whispered.

Jill smoothed the hair from her daughter's forehead. "Yes, but we're here now. We're together at last." She gazed at King across the table. "Everything's going to be alright."

***

Jill watched anxiously as King smoothed the paper over the glass. Merwin had worked so hard designing the logo, he'd been e-mailing King back and forth for the last two weeks, tweaking it here and there, but King hadn't wanted her to see. Wanted it to be a surprise. Of course she trusted him, knew it would be just right, but the curiosity was about to kill her. She'd even caught him talking to Stacey and Shawn about it behind her back. Every time she asked for a hint though, he'd just smile, shake his head, and advise patience.

He'd say, "You know that's in the Bible"

"What's in the Bible? Keeping things a secret?"

He didn't rise to the bait. "No. Patience."

She rolled her eyes and put them back on the road. He went back to texting.

"You want to drive?" She tried.

His thumbs flew, he didn't even look up. "Nope. I'm good. I can take over in a bit if'n you're tired."

He slanted a grin her way.

She sniffed. "It's barely been 60 miles. Who are you texting?"

He laughed outright. How she loved his laugh, but it still rankled that he wouldn't tell her about the logo. "Patience, My Dear. You'll see soon enough.'

But soon hadn't come quick enough and now two weeks later he'd picked up a large flat package that had been hand delivered by his truck driver friend who also happened to be an artist and led her out to the truck.

Finished, he stepped back, the paper backing of the vinyl decal dangling from his hand. Jill stepped up close and he wrapped his arm around her shoulders. She leaned in, thankfulness for this wonderful man nearly bringing tears to her eyes as they stared at the custom decal. Her heart full to bursting. Surreptitiously she wiped at her eyes, not wanting King to think she was disappointed. But just like always he sensed her mood and peered down at her.

"You don't like it?"

His voice seemed a little strained so she smiled to put his doubt to rest. She squeezed his waist. "I love it, King. It's perfect. Merwin did a great job on the design." Two stylized hearts, side by side but entwined and leaning forward as though moving took up most of the back window. The name of the new company, Second Chance Trucking arched above.

Jill sighed and leaned against her lanky cowboy. He relaxed against her they admired the logo, hearts full. How could she thank God enough for this wonderful man? Despite the terrible past that had thrown them together in the trucking company, a last ditch effort for both of them to avoid life, here they were, side by side, secure in the love they had for each other and the love that God had for him.

She squeezed harder, closing her eyes as the tears threatened again. You are not going to cry, she told herself, you are not going to ruin this perfect moment.

King shifted. "You're not having second thoughts are you?"

"No way, Cowboy. I'm just—" she sniffed. "—so happy. So thankful to God for everything, I'm feeling so blessed. I have you. I have my daughter and son. He's given me everything I thought I would never have." She gazed up into blue eyes. They sparkled down at her.

"I know, Sunshine."

She loved how he called her that. It always reminded her of when he had confessed his love and how she brought the light to his life. She prayed she always would.

He cleared his throat. "I'd never thought I'd be

this happy again. I'd have never believe that God had something so sweet in store for me here at the end of my life."

She gave him a little push. "End of your life, my foot. Here we are, starting a new company, a new life together. Don't look at this as an ending. This is just the beginning. So don't get comfortable. I have plans."

"Plans?"

"Oh yes, we haven't even been North. We need loads to Montana, places like Mount Rushmore, then there's always West—like Yellowstone. Don't you want to put your toes in the ocean? See some whales? Didn't Sam say there was a manufacturer in Washington—"

King swooped down and kissed her quick before she could draw another breath. "Okay. I get the picture. No slowing down for this ol' cowboy."

She pretend glared at him and sniffed. "Old. You're not old, not the way you run around and rescue damsels in distress."

"Well, I'll rescue *you* anytime anyhow."

Jill turned back to the truck. "You ready to hit the road?"

"Sure, load up, Gal."

She took one last look around at the Sea2Sea yard, sending a quick prayer to God for this small stretch of road in her life. It might have been bumpy, frightening, heart rending, but here she was, embarking on a brand new adventure with her cowboy by her side and God in the lead.

Epilogue

Sam watched the happy couple pull out of the yard, unable to help the sappy smile pasted on his face like a sick clown. He loved happy endings, especially when it involved his best friend who had been hurting for far too long. The long reaching arm of God's love always amazed him. He saw people miles and lifetimes apart and brought them together at just the right time for healing. King and Jill were all God's doing, no one else's, though he did enjoy being the vessel. Sam sighed and settled back in his chair, shuffling through the tall pile of applications on his desk.

Each week before choosing those that would

come to training he prayed over the pile, just like he would today. He asked that God guide his choices. That the people who needed this job would end up with it. Sam leaned forward eagerly. What kind of adventures did God still have waiting in this pile? More love matches? More healed souls? He picked the phone and started pulling out those he had marked, eager to see what God had in store.

DEAR READER

Releasing a book is a work of love that takes hundreds of hours. As an independent author it is always a wonderful thing to hear from readers. If you enjoy my work and would like to see more from me in the future, there are a couple of things you can do to help: leaving a review and recommending my book.

Leaving an Amazon review is a great help to an author. It shows other readers that you've enjoyed the book and will encourage them to try it as well. Be it one sentence or a couple of pages, I appreciate them all.

If you would like to sign up for my newsletter, visit me at www.lirabrannon.com

BONUS MATERIAL

In writing a book there are always scenes that have to be cut—no matter how much you like them. Following are two scenes from Jill and King's former lives that give a little more insight into their characters.

Jill is like many women, trapped in a dead-end job, under paid and under appreciated, however, a letter from her daughter gives her the impetus to escape.

King thought he had it made. He had a great wife, a kid he adored, all that lacked was a little extra cash to make their lives more comfortable. Despite the dangers, he signs on as a contract driver and heads to Iraq. There he receives news that changes his life forever.

Enjoy!!

So long

"That's it, I quit. After fifteen years of doing the work of three people as well as your job, I've had it. You can take this job and stick it–" Jill cut off her inner rant with a click of her mental teeth before some unchristian-like words leaped from her head to her mouth. Besides, that's not what she said anyway.

The tax papers crackled, her fingers tightened in a death grip. "Excuse me?" She managed as courteously as possible. Politeness to difficult customers is what had kept her job secure when so many others had come and gone. People such as Chad Cumberland, the slightly sadistic manager of Cumberland's Bee Supply where she worked as secretary, CPA, and gopher. All for a dollar more than minimum wage.

She fought to focus on the man's lips—knowing he was talking, but what did it matter? In a few minutes, she'd never have to see him again.

"I know you had your heart set on getting the manager position when we opened the new Arkansas branch, but I thought you should know it's been given to Neil."

Okay, this got her attention. "Neil?"

Her boss nodded. "You know, my cousin, Neil Cumberland, they gave it to him. He owns the Sweet Bee Honey Farm."

Her jaw clenched and she leaned forward to give him the papers. "Yes, I know Neil." Well, sort of. She'd met him at the company Christmas party. What she couldn't figure is why Chad would tell her this today–when her next step would be to walk out the door forever. It made no sense except that he had a subtle cruel streak she'd become well acquainted with over the last five years.

Her leaving just ticked him off is all. Throwing a tantrum because nothing he did would stop her. Her course was set. Of course, he planned to get in as many digs as he could before she actually walked out the door. She'd given him plenty of warning, even the exact date that would be her last. It wasn't her fault he hadn't listened.

He propped his feet up on the walnut desk, sending up a homey lemon scent from the polish she used last Sunday, then changed his mind and lunged forward to snatch the papers. Long years with him was the only thing that saved her from flinching. She guessed ages ago he thought such aggressive posturings were cool and it was best not to show any reaction one way or another.

His flat eyes touched on her face briefly before fixating on the clock above the door behind her. "You're sure about this? You're actually leaving?"

"Yes." For the past year she'd planned this step by step. Dreamed about it, half frightened, half excited, but definitely going through with it. She'd been passed over for promotion every year for the last five years. Of course, she'd expected it.

"You know I've already hired umm--"

She refrained from rolling her eyes. "Margie."

"Yes, Margie. I don't know if I could make room for you if you change your mind."

"Thanks, but that's okay." Besides, after being passed over so many times, there was no where else for her to go but out the door.

When it came to moving up in the company, everyone knew the Cumberlands kept everything in the family. The male part that is. Soon a whole new generation would hit the work force, leaving more hard working assistants, like her, out in the cold. Maybe even a Cumberland would've been better than Chad. For five years now he'd been the Ark-La-Tex branch head while Jill managed. He spent most of the work day playing solitaire on the computer.

Sure, he had the degree, but Jill knew a whole lot more about running a branch office of the bee supplier than he did. Even in these tough times, Cumberland's Bee Supply customer base had grown due to her calls and persistence of excellence from warehouse to shipping. It was her templates, developed after years of rewriting the same letters hundreds of times, that the whole company used. She who dealt with the main office about taxes, insurance, and international shipping orders–not Chad.

What would the powers above do when they realized he didn't have a clue about even the most basic of office functions? He'd never even logged into the invoice system until a week ago when it became certain she wouldn't change her mind about leaving.

"Make sure Margie's got everything before you take off then. And leave the key."

She nodded with a hard jerk, gritting her teeth. "Of course."

When it became clear that's all he had to say, she turned and left the office.

She glanced around the open front area with the displays of beekeeping books, a hooded manikin, and various equipment, looking for something to do. Stalling. She'd already closed out the cash drawer and filled out the deposit slip. She'd dusted the display of smokers and hive bodies and adjusted the how-to books so the spines aligned perfectly with the edge of the maple shelf. The mail sat in neat piles for tomorrow's pick up. Out of habit, she flicked the thermostat down to 60 degrees for the night. Though April, the fickle Texas weather had a bite that called for the heat during business hours.

She re-read the e-mail sent to all the customers she'd grown close to over the last fifteen years, explaining that all questions should be directed to Margie or Chad. That should prove interesting, considering that both knew next to nothing about the items in the warehouse. Chad was a textbook of bee knowledge, he should be having grown up tending them, but when it came to dealing with the customers, he dropped the ball.

Those finding Chad difficult to deal with always turned to her and she'd made many friends through Cumberland's extensive network. Interpreting Chad's knowledgeable, though cryptic solutions to beekeeper issues had introduced her to a variety of interesting people that came to rely on her.

Boy, would she miss them. Even cranky Mrs. Sanderfeld, now 86 and still tending her own hives, called saying "I wanna talk to Jill." Many had offered her a place to stay while she traveled the country with her new job and she just might take a few up on their invitations. She smiled to think about it. No more sitting behind a desk fighting with the ancient cash register and a drawer that wouldn't open unless given a whack. No, Margie could deal with that. She'd be delivering RVs and anything else with four wheels from manufacturer to final destinations all over the country.

Jill sighed and caught the eye of the new office worker. "Well, Margie, it's all yours." Poor thing. She'd been hired by Chad just two days ago, even with the six month notice she'd given and the constant hints to hire someone.

Margie patted her computer. "Don't worry, I've got this."

Jill stared at the sixty-something woman with gray hair and 200 extra pounds who struggled in and out of the chair. How she would do? This job required a lot of running back and forth to check inventory in the back when Rich and Tina, the warehouse workers, were busy shipping or packing.

She took a steadying breath. "I'm glad to hear it."

The office sat still, as though holding it's breath to keep her back before the compulsion to breath again expelled her forever. Margie's rasping exhales competed with the squeak of the ceiling fan. The little hand ticked 20 minutes after five. Why linger? The two warehouse workers had left and Margie waited for her ride. She couldn't guess why Chad stayed. He rarely showed his face back in the office after he picked up his kids.

Suddenly itching to get out of there and get started, she gathered her purse and sweater. The time had come.

Chad wandered out of his office, eyes touched her face then slid away. "Are you gonna eat your cake?"

Stymied Jill looked at him. "What cake?" There had been a cake in the refrigerator, the one Rich picked up at lunch for his kid's birthday. The black and white confection definitely hadn't been hers though, it had *Happy Birthday, Tyler* written on it with a soccer ball and a freckle faced goalie.

"Yours, it's been sitting there all day. Who'd you think it was for?" Jill bit her tongue again, something she had done a lot over the last five years. It's a wonder she could talk past the callus that had formed.

She stared at Chad, still at a loss. "Okaay, I don't know what you mean."

Her boss ran his hand through his hair and sighed. "Come on."

She followed him around the pitted desk, hers since the day she'd applied for the job, to the little break room that smelled of microwave burritos and stale coffee. Someone hadn't emptied the day's joe again. It sat like road tar in the chipped pot with a consistency that should work wonders on the pot hole infested parking lot.

Chad pointed to the top of the ice box. "Right there."

Jill eyed the edge of the apartment sized cooler, perched like a hippopotamus on a rickety card table, and shook her head. Honestly? Chad stood an easy six feet with a lanky build that belied his sedentary lifestyle. Even in her sneakers, five feet was still an inch away. The top of the refrigerator, any refrigerator, was uncharted territory without a step ladder.

He took down a small dessert, hardly bigger than a petit four. It looked a little worse for wear from sitting on top of the refrigerator instead of in it and subject to a blast of heat every time someone opened the warehouse door. The chocolate shavings looked like a pen had exploded against the clear plastic. The whipped cream frosting listed like a snow heavy Christmas tree, sure to fall when she opened the top.

He thrust it into her hands. "Here you go. Congratu—Happy trails."

Keep calm. Pasting the smile she reserved for 'special' customers–and Chad–she fingered the plastic base. "You shouldn't have." Tears seeped against her lids and she blinked them back, glad her thick glasses and Chad's height prevented him from seeing her weakness. Now was not the time for a pity party.

What did she expect anyway? A gold watch? A going away party? This is how they did things around here. The old 'take your cake and git' method. She should have left when the branch changed managers, after the first two passes for promotion. Why didn't I leave? But she knew. Memories surged. Ribs aching with each breath, the coppery taste of blood in her mouth. She shoved them away and focused on Chad.

His lips moved. It took her a moment for the words to sink in. "Thank Tina and Margie. It was their idea. I bought it Monday, but forgot about it."

Lovely. Today was Friday, maybe the decorations weren't candy bits, maybe they're penicillin.

Chad stepped back, obviously uncomfortable. "Well then." He turned and bolted towards the main office and the safety of Margie's presence.

Jill looked at the cake then followed him, fighting the urge to throw it at the back of his head. But she didn't.

It wasn't his fault after all. She should have spoken her mind when he shoved more and more work on her, demanding she stay late for inventory alone instead of asking Tina and Rich to help. She should have protested when he fired the janitors and told her to fill in until he found a new crew, with no extra pay of course. He never did. He'd pocketed the extra sent by the home office for cleaning. In everything she'd kept silent—too frightened to leave. Afraid of everything.

She'd needed the job so badly, first after the divorce, then getting Shawn through school, and then when Stacey had gone to prison–stop it. No time to think of Stacey right now. Anyway, no more of that. No more fear, no more waiting for her life to begin. She straightened her shoulders. No more taking the easy route—moving on.

She raised her brows at the other office worker. "Margie, would you like a couple of pieces for you and Harold?"

The gray haired woman shifted to a more comfortable position, sympathy for Jill making her faded blue eyes sparkle with kindness. "Sure, if you have enough."

Jill nodded, keeping an unladylike snort to herself. Who exactly would she share it with? She returned to the break room, cut the cake and put one half on a paper plate. She covered it with plastic wrap, cleaned the knife, and put everything away. She even emptied that stinking pot of coffee.

Jill returned to the main room with the two pieces of cake and watched Margie lever herself out of the chair. Her husband, Harold, stood in the doorway, waiting to help his wife down the three front steps and out to the car. She followed her replacement's slow progress across the room and handed Harold the cake. He was a small, bird-like man. A stark comparison to the wife he doted on.

He took the plate from her. "Thanks, kiddo. So you're hitting the road. Footloose and fancy free, eh?"

Jill nodded and forced a smile. "Yep, that's me."

"Got the kid grown and now you can do what you want, eh?"

Again she nodded, fighting down the panic that rose every time someone mentioned her kid. The word was kid, not the plural. Few knew she had two offspring and she meant to keep it that way.

She took a breath through her nose. "Yes, I'm headed out tomorrow for Indiana. Driver's training starts Monday and I should be out with my first load by Wednesday afternoon."

The older man patted her shoulder. "Well, that's just fine. You be careful on the road now, there are all kinds of kooks out there."

Margie slapped him playfully. "Don't go scarin' her with all your horror stories." She cut a glance at Jill as though worried his words would frighten her. As if.

Belatedly, she remembered Harold had once been a truck driver. "Oh, don't worry about me. This is a great company and I've got it all planned out: places where I can stop, eat, everything. I have lots of friends all over who've offered me a place to stay while I'm in their neighborhood too."

Harold nodded. "As long as you don't break down in the middle of nowhere."

Jill laughed at his dark warning. "I'll be driving mostly new units, or close to it. The company'll put me up in a hotel and pay me down time if I do breakdown. There's someone available 24 hours to call if there's trouble. I'll be fine. You guys enjoy that cake now and take care."

She ushered the couple out the door. Returning to her desk, she placed the master keys in the top drawer, and grabbed her purse. One last look around the room she had built her life around for so long. The dark paneling from the '80s brooded back at her. Who would call pest control when the termites swarmed again? She shrugged. Not her problem anymore.

She thought of all the people that had come in and out of the office over the years, all the friends she had made, but underneath all the friendships she had to admit she'd been lonely. Lonely for that helpmate designed just for her.

Why hadn't God sent her that special someone she longed for? The divorce had been nine years ago. Since then she'd meant dozens and dozens of *eligible* men, but none had ignited the tiniest spark of interest. Maybe she was meant to be alone, like Paul in the Bible. Maybe God had other things in mind for her than a happily ever after and growing old with some man.

Jill shook her head. I'm stalling. I just need to step out in faith. I know that God has a plan for me beyond this stagnant place. I'll not be tied down with a house and bills anymore.

With the decision to let God guide her life, Jill felt a gentle sense of peace calm the anxiety that had been eating at her and making her jumpy and caustic. It didn't matter that everything she'd ever owned was in storage or packed into her car. This would be an adventure and God would be her guide. The animosity and resentment towards Chad and the Cumberlands winged away as she took a deep breath. No doubts now, this dead end cave was the past. Her future awaited on the interstates of America. She just had to get out that portal.

Without looking back, Jill placed her hand on the door and with a little prayer, stepped out into the soft evening light of the Texas spring, ready, Lord willing, to move on with her life.

BAD NEWS

He sat in the JRD trucker's lounge in Iraq, chilling with Greasy Jack and Killjoy after a harrowing run. A booby trapped donkey carcass had come close to sending Bible Thumper into the arms of his maker. His God had an eye on him though, because he ended up in the hospital with cute nurses fussing over a couple of broken ribs and a head wound, while three soldiers of the protection detail cooled in the morgue.

King didn't hold with preaching your beliefs at everyone, and especially not since Carol had run off with her Holy Roller. But nothing stopped Bible Thumper. He meant to save every soul around him, Muslims included, a habit that had gotten him shot at a few times. Then again, it could be that great big crucifix dangling from his review mirror he *had* to kiss every time he got in his truck. Like cross hairs for the snipers, it gave them something to aim as as they sat on the buildings taking pot shots at the drivers.

The young Pentecostal from Idaho had his whole life ahead of him, why he wanted to die so badly that he made himself a daily target King couldn't figure. Still, the kid had been part of the team. Those that had returned in one piece gathered to toast his quick recovery. With any luck, the company would send him back stateside and leave the rest of the crew to wallow in their sins.

An earlier power outage had warmed the beer, but the alcohol dulled the edge of the memories and bloody bodies lying in the ditch alongside the donkey's. It washed the sand down his throat, a brief respite from the constant sandpaper feel. He hacked and spat in the paper cup on his left.

The run had been one of the usual. Stop for nothing, drive like the devil knocked on the back doors, and let the soldiers take care of insurgents.

But the protection detail ended up crawling in the ditch, searching for cover that would never be found. One kid lay next to his own leg, blood pumping out in a puddle.

King gunned his engine and flew by, cowboy hat hitting the top of the cab as he ran over rubble and God knew what else. Even an unbeliever like him sent off a short prayer in times like that, hoping to God it wasn't a body part of someone he knew under those man eating tires.

He jerked the beer to his lips and grimaced as the sweetness pushed the sour bile back where it belonged.

Greasy Jack raised his bottle. Killjoy and King touched it with theirs. "To Bible Thumper." A chorus of "to Thumper" and "to Bible Boy" and the occasional "Joe" sounded around the room. *Was his name Joe?* It amazed him anyone even knew it. The kid had started preaching from day one so the crew had dubbed him Bible Thumper. The crazy boy had liked it too.

Sam Vick, dispatcher and go-to man

extraordinaire, motioned to him from behind the partition they used to give him the privacy of an office.

He stood and leaned over the wall, careful of the tacks holding the 'Do Not Disturb the Crab' sign. "Hey Sam, what's up?"

The dispatcher, usually a painful shade of red from the unrelenting sun and heat, didn't return the smile. In fact, he looked a couple of shades paler and his eyes shifted uneasily instead of his usual direct gaze. He shook his head, half turning to his computer, then, deciding differently, turned back and motioned him to come all the way in. "Sit down, Cowboy. This just sucks, and I'm sorry, there's just no easy way to break this to you. The Kenyan government wants to get ahold of you."

King didn't know what to say. "Okaaaay," he finally drawled. He sat in the proffered metal folding chair, wondering what kind of joke his buddies had cooked up. The drivers tried to keep life light here, as best as they could anyway, but Sam usually stood aloft from their antics.

The other man ran a hand over his balding pate. "They have some bodies they need you to identify."

He nearly spewed his beer all over the supervisor. "Me? Bodies in Kenya?" Okay, this joke just might be over the top, especially if they have Sam involved.

The man flushed red and jerked back to the computer. "Yeah, prepare yourself. I. . . I think it's Carol--maybe Waylon."

King's anticipation of a good punch line turned to dread. His mind spun and finally latched onto what could be a piece of this jigsaw puzzle. Carol's good-bye letter. A short missive tucked in with the divorce papers. What had he done with it? Burned it? He liked to burn things when he got mad. Hadn't it said she was headed to Africa? Was Kenya in Africa?

Images flashed onto the screen, spearing into his brain like the dots that formed behind closed eyelids after looking directly into the sun. A young blonde boy, body slumped against a mud wall, a single bullet in his forehead. Carol—Oh, God, Carol

—what had happened to Carol was defied imagination. How could anyone even think of doing those sorts of things? She might be a low down cheat, but no one, no one deserved that.

The world spun. He'd seen bad things before, just some of the stuff on the side of the road in Iraq would give any man nightmares, but this was different. This was his son, his baby boy.

He turned and puked, barely making it into the plastic wastebasket. Then he collapsed, a heaving mess of Texas cowboy, snot, and tears on Sam's meaty shoulder.

ABOUT THE AUTHOR

Lira Brannon lives on a hill in Texas where everything truly is bigger—including bugs and dreams. Writing has always been a part of her life, except for a brief time of insanity when she thought she should become a pharmacist. She writes in several genres including award winning short stories, as well as Picture Books, Romance, and Young Adult.

Follow Lira to find out what's coming next:

www.lirabrannon.com

www.pinterest.com/lirabrannon/

https://twitter.com/Lislann

www.facebook.com/LBrannonAuthor

www.amazon.com/Lira-Brannon/